P9-BZJ-675

PRAISE FOR THE
INSPECTOR KENWORTHY MYSTERIES
BY JOHN BUXTON HILTON

"Full of suspense and atmosphere!" —*Library Journal*

"Begins with a sensational case that immediately is topped with another shocker . . . Hilton has crafted a solid mystery!" —*Washington Post*

"Entertaining . . . A taut, intriguing little puzzle." —*Kirkus*

"Satisfying and plausible . . . a dramatic climax!" —*Publishers Weekly*

"Complex, keen, and suspenseful." —*Booklist*

"Hilton's sophisticated writing has lifted his novels out of the traditional mystery genre and won him growing critical renown . . . Intriguing!" —*Mystery News*

"An unusual, offbeat style."—*The Oxford Eagle* (Miss.)

"Holds the reader's attention . . . Thought-provoking and very interesting." —*Kansas City Star*

Books by John Buxton Hilton

HANGMAN'S TIDE
FATAL CURTAIN
PLAYGROUND OF DEATH
CRADLE OF CRIME
HOLIDAY FOR MURDER
DEAD MAN'S PATH

DEAD MAN'S PATH

JOHN BUXTON HILTON

Originally published as *Death of an Alderman*

DIAMOND BOOKS, NEW YORK

This book was originally published
in Great Britain by Cassell & Company Ltd.
under the title *Death of an Alderman*.

DEAD MAN'S PATH

A Diamond Book / published by arrangement with
the author's estate

PRINTING HISTORY
Cassell & Company Ltd edition published 1968
Chivers Press edition published 1987
Diamond edition / February 1992

ISBN: 1-55773-662-6

Diamond Books are published by The Berkley Publishing Group,
200 Madison Avenue, New York, New York 10016.
The name "DIAMOND" and its logo are trademarks
belonging to Charter Communications, Inc.

PRINTED IN THE UNITED STATES OF AMERICA

10 9 8 7 6 5 4 3 2 1

• 1 •

FOR FIFTEEN MILES there was scarcely a break between the conurbations. Steep streets of terraced houses swept up from the railway embankment, clustering round the red brick Victorian mills that they served. Now and then pit-head gear rose stark and primitive, and here and there the slag-heaps gave way to the coarse grass of hills that bulged away in overlapping folds to the moors of the horizon.

Detective-Superintendent Simon Kenworthy looked down at a brook spanned by a wooden foot-bridge.

"Before the industrial revolution, Shiner, this must have been rather a lovely county."

Sergeant Wright looked up from his unsatisfying paperback. It was a relief that the old man was taking a pleasurable interest in his surroundings. Kenworthy was notoriously a Londoner and could be difficult company in the provinces.

The superintendent made a fresh fold in his Ordnance Survey map and studied the landscape.

"That must be the canal in question—"

Flanked by an infrequently trodden towpath, a waterway ran parallel to the train for some two hundred yards, then curved away behind the suburban gardens of a post-war housing estate.

"It must be somewhere along there that they found him."

"And that must be the ruin where they found the gun."

For a moment they caught sight of a hulk of broken walls beside a stone bridge, and then the train was clasped in a cutting of dripping brown gritstone which sucked them into a short, sooty tunnel. Even before daylight began to lighten the smoke-caked brick-work, the brakes began to clamp the wheels. The two men gathered their bags from the rack.

The station at Fellaby was crudely unendearing. Black puddles of recent rain swamped the platform. To reach the *Exit* side they had to go down through a dank subway lit by a single incandescent gas mantle. In the small forecourt the driver of the only taxi was standing with his door held expectantly open.

"We'll walk," Kenworthy said, despite their cases, and ignoring the rain, which was beginning again.

"The police-station's on the other side of town."

"To hell with the police-station. Let's have a look round with our own eyes, before they hamper us with half a dozen guides."

They stopped at the first intersection of streets and studied the façades of a mill and a non-conformist chapel, both abandoned, and a row of depressed shops.

"And it said in the *Notes*," Wright commented, "that the place is remarkable for its civic pride."

"'Where there's muck there's money'—that's a basic idea that has entered into their souls. It hasn't occurred to them yet that a town can be both prosperous and clean."

Kenworthy led the way into a newsagent's and asked for a local paper.

"Do you want the *Gazette* or the *Herald*?"

"Both."

"The *Herald* only comes out on Tuesdays—that was before—"

The man behind the counter had weighed them up for what they were.

Borough Alderman Murdered: Wright caught sight of the headline before Kenworthy picked up and folded the paper, and beneath it a head and shoulders portrait of the deceased, affluent, faintly smiling, proud—and rather too flabby for his thirty-five years.

"You'll need your own copies," Kenworthy said.

"The *Gazette,* then."

"I should get both, if I were you. See what they found to say about this town when it was normal."

Wright had not worked with Kenworthy before, and he had been plied with many stories of the superintendent's mild eccentricities, one of which was an exasperatingly leisurely approach to pending urgencies.

At the *County Hotel* he had his first significant experience of this. The sergeant wasted no time after being shown his bedroom. He hurried back into the lounge with the least possible delay, but it was a full half hour before the superintendent came down the broad, floral carpeted staircase, as unhurriedly as if he were on holiday. Wright leaped to his feet, but Kenworthy waved him good-humouredly back to his arm-chair and opened out one of the newspapers, which he still carried under his arm.

"Make anything of it, Shiner?"

"Conventional reportage—family man—three kids—got on well at a pretty early age. Finger in plenty of pies. Must have had influential friends. J.P., too, I notice, and chairman of the juvenile bench. Must have made an enemy or two, as well, I suppose—"

"As you say—influential friends. His rise in this particular political party has been what you might call meteoric for someone born on the wrong side of the tracks."

"Wrong side of the tracks?"

Kenworthy tapped the *Gazette* with the back of his knuckles.

"'Born in Kenilworth Street'—I took the trouble to have a good look at the town map on the way up here. Kenilworth Street backs down to the goods-yard. And 'son of Edward Barson, weaver'—that doesn't add up, either."

"Oh, I don't know," Wright said. "This is the 1960's. A man who has it about him—"

"Can get on to the local council in his early twenties? Granted. Can get on to the magisterial and aldermanic benches in next to no time? Possibly. He may have had a magnetic personality. To judge from these—"

Kenworthy indicated a whole page of photographs: Barson visiting the children's hospital on Christmas morning, Barson opening a Garden Fête, Barson speaking at a Rotary Charter Night, Barson laying the foundation stone of an extension to the public library.

"Believe me, Shiner—I know towns like this. There are dodderers in their dotage queueing up for this sort of honour. I'm not saying it's definitely phoney f-to horn in. But it'll bear looking into—especially when it's a weaver's lad from Kenilworth Street.—Make anything of the other rag?"

Wright picked up the *Herald*.

"There seems to have been an acrimonious correspondence going on between Barson and the other side."

"You mean Councillor Durkin's letter?"

For a man who seemed asleep three quarters of the time, Kenworthy had a surprising command of detail.

"Yes, Durkin's letter. But it's all speculation about what went on at Suez. That was years ago. It's nothing to do with Fellaby."

"These people like to sling mud about. Probably both Durkin and Barson fancy themselves a parliamentary constituency. They like to keep their names in print. Anything else?"

"No. Barson seems to have had a fairly quiet week."

Kenworthy pointed to a column.

"Nasty court case. Juvenile delinquent sent to Borstal for about his twentieth offence. It doesn't say Barson was in the chair, but I think we can take that for granted. And this is the sort of hoodlum who's sure to have left some bloody-minded pals behind. Again, it'll bear looking into, though I'm sure the local boys will have covered it."

He looked at his watch.

"And speaking of the local boys—I don't think we can put the evil moment off much longer—"

Yet even as they walked across the town, Kenworthy stopped again. He explained that his wife set store by the picture postcards which he had been sending home for years from the various towns where he had handled cases. And he spent as much time over them as if they had been rare reproductions for a connoisseur, though there were only three to choose from: the High Street, the parish church and the war memorial.

"Besides, Shiner, we've got to get to know this town. We've got to know it better than the oldest inhabitant does."

The police-station was a forbidding, overcrowded, late nineteenth-century building, situated in that part of the town which was the preserve of Georgian fronted solicitors', accountants' and estate agents' offices. Kenworthy and

Wright were shown into an upstairs room whose scrubbed wooden boards and metal filing cabinets were scarcely relieved by a pocket handkerchief of worn red carpet.

Chief superintendent Grayling, who commanded the Fellaby Division, was a tall, lean, austere man, disciplined through and through. Not spectacularly imaginative, Wright thought, but undoubtedly adept at carrying out the letter of the law without offending local society.

"Meet my deputy—"

This was a uniformed chief inspector called Dunne, who had the jowls of a hearty beer drinker, and who evidently enjoyed every moment of his work, for he punctuated his cynical comments with resonant guffaws, and it was clear that he had an inexhaustible capacity for anecdote.

Grayling lifted the house-phone.

"Detective superintendent Rhys, from County HQ, has made himself responsible for the Report Centre—which, incidentally, we've set up in the Congregational Sunday School."

Kenworthy's eyes clouded momentarily, and Grayling permitted himself a faint smile. It was as if he had heard that other men smiled, and had taught himself to go through the motions.

"All right, superintendent—we have been warned: you don't like Report Centres—"

"It isn't that I don't like them. We couldn't get far without them, at the present pace of living. It's just that I like to feel free—"

"Don't worry, superintendent. You won't be nailed down. You can confidently leave the routine to Rhys. And I may say—"

There followed the expected build-up for the county man, the assurances of a hundred percent support, the inevitable reserves about the shortages of transport and manpower.

"While we're waiting for Rhys," Kenworthy suggested, "perhaps you'd fill us in on the general stuff—Fellaby Borough Council, now. What does it really amount to?"

Dunne did not wait for his chief to invite him to answer.

"A market," he said, "lighting the streets and occasionally sweeping them. A public health department, a sewage farm and a cemetery. A park, three housing estates, a library and a museum. A swimming bath in the summer and slipper baths all the year round. A few miles of secondary road. An education committee—"

"Relic of the day," Grayling interposed, "when they ran their own schools. Nowadays it merely appoints representatives to other bodies."

"Likewise a watch committee—"

"Relic of the borough police force, which the county took over in the 1930's. Nowadays it does no more than express opinions—"

Dunne produced one of his gigantic laughs.

"And it collects reports from dirty old man who crawl about the park with cross-channel binoculars and then express surprise at what they see."

"And a lot of property," Grayling added quickly, "most of it let on long lease. The corporation owns a large proportion of the town."

"And Barson's part in all this?"

"Chairman of Markets, Vice-chairman of Library, member of Housing, Health and Finance."

Kenworthy took out his pipe and filled its bowl meditatively.

"It doesn't amount to much, does it?" he said. "I mean, viewed globally."

"You wouldn't think so, if you saw the cut-throat competition to get these positions."

"Conservative controlled?"

"Only just. The constituency, which is bigger than the borough, went Labour for the first time at the last election. But there's been no change in the borough up to now—though, oddly enough, the new shuffle might just turn the balance. Nobody's dared to say it in public yet, but Barson's death gives the other side high hopes."

Kenworthy struck a match.

"It seems pretty petty to me. They say power corrupts—but what can come out of power on this little patch?—Forgive me, superintendent—but what could there be in it for a wrong 'un? Five quid for the best market site? A joint of meat for not seeing the flies on the slab? Cross my palm and go up in the housing list?"

"Nothing like that," Grayling said. "There hasn't been

such a case in my memory. And if the democrats were vulnerable, I'd stake my reputation on the integrity of the officials. We've a town clerk with an eye like a hawk. I'll swear nothing would get past him."

"Of course—Barson didn't stop at borough politics—"

"Director of the Town Football Club—"

"J.P.," Kenworthy added.

"Set a thief to catch a thief," Dunne said, and Grayling looked as if he would have liked to apologise for him. But at that moment Rhys knocked and joined them.

He was a bigly built Welshman, scrupulously careful in his speech, anxious not to appear incompetent in the Yard man's presence. Kenworthy made no attempt to put him at his ease.

"I've read everything you sent by teleprinter, but it would be as well to run quickly over everything."

"Barson always took his dog for a walk last thing at night, generally along the towpath of a canal on the edge of the estate where he lives.—The Carlton Estate.—Rather expensive—"

" 'The Debtors' Retreat,' " Dunne said.

"On the night of 23rd February, between 9:45 and 9:50, he was shot dead, at close quarters, with a Luger pistol. The dog was also shot."

"No witnesses?"

"One or two neighbours saw him set out. No one saw any other character."

"Someone must have heard the shots."

"Nearly everyone on the estate. But no one went out. Too keen on the telly, I suppose. A routine patrol came from nearly a mile away. Barson was dead when he arrived."

"The Luger?"

"Had been on exhibition in a collection of trophies given by local men to the borough museum. This had been broken into the previous night, between midnight and two a.m. Investigation has so far drawn a blank."

"You found the weapon?"

"The morning after the crime, in a derelict warehouse about a quarter of a mile from the murder spot. Also various bits and pieces belonging to an adolescent gang that was known to use the ruin as a sort of headquarters."

"And," Kenworthy prompted, "the leader of this gang had been sent to Borstal the previous week?"

"That is correct."

"By Barson?"

"That is so."

"Leaving how many associates still at large?"

"None that we consider dangerous—though a few who might be noisy—including the ring-leader's brother, a nineteen year old, Chick Stanway."

"Whom you've questioned?"

"We've had him in. Big-mouthed, truculent—but soft. Been shooting his mouth off about what he'd do to Barson, ever since his brother was sentenced. But there's no material evidence to connect him with the crime."

"But you could find a holding charge, if you wanted?"

"On suspicion on at least half a dozen files. But we think, if he's involved at all, that he's more likely to incriminate himself outside than he is in a cell."

Rhys came triumphantly to his dramatic climax.

"A much more interesting feature has emerged from our house-to-house questionnaires. It appears that during the week before the murder, some character was going round the town—particularly round the Carlton Estate—asking questions about Barson—his movements, his habits, his associates—anything he could trip people into telling him."

"You've a good description?"

"Including Identikit."

Rhys removed a sheet from a folder and passed it to Kenworthy.

"Not a local man?"

"Positively not. And he operated in the guise of one of these door-to-door religious cranks—working in a few crafty questions about the neighbours."

"Get it out for maximum coverage as soon as you can. The press will enjoy it.—'The man with the feather in his hat'—"

Rhys made a note.

"That's about all—"

"This gives us one lead outside Fellaby," Kenworthy said. "Where else had Barson ever been?"

"He did national service. He was too young for the war

itself but he was in Germany afterwards. Corporal in the R.A.S.C."

"Sergeant Wright.—Have that covered for us, will you?—And his job? What did that amount to? 'Advertising executive' might mean anything."

Grayling spoke for the first time since Rhys had started his exposition.

"Whatever it means, it enabled him to have a better standard of living than a chief superintendent—and to devote all the time he wanted to committee work. As far as I've ever been able to ascertain, he was a sort of middleman between advertisers and copy-writers. He sold space and then commissioned material to fill it."

"What was his firm?"

"*Futurco Publicity*. Headquarters in Bradcaster. They have all the poster space in the Bradcaster buses, as well as a strong following in periodicals and local papers."

Kenworthy turned to Rhys.

"Put someone on to that. We want every angle of his *Futurco* activities—his contacts, his women—everything—"

"Very good, superintendent. Would you like to come over and see the Report Centre now?"

Kenworthy suppressed a sigh and allowed himself to be led over to the tactical headquarters. He showed a polite interest in the telephone switchboard, the uniformed constables sorting statements, the minute-to-minute log of messages and operational orders.

"This will be your desk."

Kenworthy tried to hide his distaste as he looked down at the article of green metal, regulation furniture.

"Let's hope I shan't find too much use for it. Just now my main desire is to take a walk along the High Street before the shops close. You can come with me, Sergeant Wright."

But outside, he gave his sergeant a different instruction.

"Shiner—I want you to run the rule over that museum break-in. Try to make out whether it was an amateur or professional job."

· 2 ·

WRIGHT SPENT A few minutes on the telephone, initiating enquiries into Barson's army background, and then he broached the question of the burglary. He was accompanied to the museum not, as he had hoped, by one of the Fellaby men of his own or inferior rank, with whom he might quickly have struck up a working comradeship, but by Malpas, a plain clothes inspector, who handed over the field report with pointed lack of comment.

The entry had been made by using sticking-plaster and a glass-cutter. It was a professional method, but one which any tyro could have picked up from detective fiction. The path outside the window was of loose gravel and had been disturbed by feet, but bore no recognisable imprints. Flaked mud had been found inside the museum, but it led to no useful conclusions. And the glass case that had contained the Luger had been broken open in the crudest possible way, its none too robust lid prised open with some sort of lever. It might have been the work of a jemmy, but a medium sized screw-driver would have done the job. There were no finger-prints.

"So you see, sergeant, even Dr. Thorndike's little box of test-tubes wouldn't have much to go on."

The museum was housed in what had formerly been an industrialist's villa, to which the library formed a modern, single-storey annexe. The collection was grotesque and had little obvious relationship with the town and its neighbourhood. A moose's head, badly stuffed and leering, presided over a wall decked with Zulu shields and assagai, and a moth-eaten badger cowered against the roughly painted

background of a hedge-bottom. The Luger had been stolen
from a side-room which contained an exhibition entitled
Fellaby at War, starting with the early compressed iron
rations of the South African campaigns, through a fully
accoutred effigy private from the Somme, to stick-grenades
and Nazi bayonet scabbards.

The curator danced attendance on them, a little, bird-like
man called Gill, who hopped about nervously, and was full
of superfluous self-exoneration.

"Of course, I blame myself, now. I had often wondered
about the wisdom of leaving such an object on show. But it
seemed a good deal more secure than some of the weapons
that could be taken by anyone with half a brick from the
gunsmith's window in town."

The broken window had been roughly covered with a
rectangle of ply-wood. Wright examined the scratches on
the sill and floor beneath it, and then asked if he might
remove the temporary covering.

"Certainly, sergeant, if you see any point in it. Every
square inch of it has been gone over, you know."

Wright brought out a clasp-knife and loosened a few
nails. The inspector stood by without offering assistance as
he lifted the thin boarding to the floor. Wright examined the
empty window-frame in prolonged silence, at one point
pinching out a tiny splinter of glass between his forefinger
and thumb.

"What's out there?" he asked. "Bushes?"

He pointed to the narrow strip of lawn beyond the outside
path, already obscured by dusk.

"Yes—and every damned spot has been gone over with a
tape-measure, lens and dog. You'll find nothing there,
sergeant."

"Good," Wright said. "I hadn't thought I would."

He began to replace the boarding, and tried to hammer
home the nails with the butt of his knife. Gill came forward.

"You can leave that to me, sergeant. I'll go upstairs
presently and fetch a hammer."

The curator was still hovering anxiously a few paces from
them. Wright marvelled at the man's fussiness, the restless-
ness of his eyes and fingers, and tension in his every
movement. He was not old—only a little over thirty—but

he was prematurely bald, slight in build, and looked like a bad novelist's caricature of a fossil-collector.

"Have we finished, sergeant?" inspector Malpas asked.

"Yes, thank you. Sorry to be such a nuisance."

"There aren't any other bits of our previous work on which you'd like to back-track?"

"I'm sorry if I've conveyed that sort of attitude, sir."

"You haven't conveyed any sort of attitude at all. All you've produced up to now is that sort of work. You'll be wanting to get back to your hotel now, I suppose?"

"I'll be wanting to report to superintendent Kenworthy, sir."

"Can you find your own way? I've had no tea, and I'm on duty tonight."

In fact, Wright was very eager indeed to find his chief, for he thought he had discovered something in the museum which ought to be reported without delay. But there was no sign of Kenworthy in the County Hotel. He was not in his bed-room, not in the dining-room, not in the lounge. The porter could not help him: if he had gone out, he had taken his room key with him. Wright walked over to the Report Centre and found the atmosphere there dispiritingly slack. A helmetless constable had a tin lid of cigarette-ends beside the idle switchboard and was now deeply absorbed in a who-dunnit. No one had seen Kenworthy since the afternoon.

Wright strolled out into the drizzle-swept heart of Fellaby and within five minutes had walked the length of the main shopping street. The sodium lighting soon gave way to a row of dingy standard lamps and the rows of shops petered out into terraces of drab-bricked houses. A gang of youths came noisily along the pavement, ready to edge into the gutter any pedestrian who happened in their way. Wright crossed to the other side of the road and began his window-shopping progress back towards the town centre. He stopped outside the window of a small tobacconist who was also advertising agency tours to Majorca and the Dolomites.

Suddenly a voice hailed him from a doorway where he could have sworn no man was standing.

"You haven't found him yet, then?"

He turned and saw a macabre cripple, a man whose left leg was so withered and twisted that it was surprising he could move about at all, crouching behind a stand loaded with sodden newspapers.

The whole town knew the man from London already. The wearisome comic scorn was beginning.

"Found him yet? You know who it is we're looking for, do you?"

The newsman spat into the night.

"I don't mean him—I mean your boss. That's who you're looking for now, isn't it?"

"Have you seen him, then?"

"He went into the *Saracen's Head* half an hour ago."

He indicated a narrow-fronted pub opposite, on which the cohort of hooligans was converging.

"Thank you."

Wright gave him a shilling for a paper that he did not want and went over to the pub. The bar had a scrubbed wooden floor, high-backed benches with tatty brown paint and layers of static cigarette smoke hanging across an atmosphere otherwise dominated by the reek of stale beer and human sweat. Most of the floor and chair space was occupied by a convention of louts of both sexes: young men with filthy clothes and sallow skin, but with immaculately washed hair that shoaled about their shoulders. And there were girls with lank blonde tresses that started from ill-concealed brunette partings and scattered dandruff about the yokes of absurdly short coats.

Wright elbowed his way across the room, taking care not to knock against any outstretched mug of ale. Kenworthy was wedged against the bar itself, talking to four of the drinkers, one of them an enormously built specimen in a stridently opulent overcoat in silver-grey imitation fur that must surely symbolise leadership of the whole gathering. The other youth was wearing a type of bottle-green, early century mid-European uniform, with meaningless epaulettes and a long row of gun-metal buttons. But his face was anything but military—pasty and spotted—with a fawning admiration for his chief which robbed him of any personality of his own. The taller of the two girls looked from behind as if she might be a worthy mate for a minor chieftain, for her hair was a golden glory, and her figure went in and out in the right places and in the right proportion. But, seen full face, her skin was coarse and bloodless, her eyes tired and devoid of intelligence, her mouth weak and dissatisfied.

The other girl was tiny, with pinkly made-up cheeks, warm brown eyes and hair neatly fringed. She was obviously deeply infatuated with the owner of the fur-coat, about whom every observable feature was gross. His hair was thick and black and grew down the side of his face in square-cut sideboards. Sweat was standing in huge beads on his forehead and trickling in runnels past his wide, fleshy nostrils. A glass containing a double whisky was almost lost against his enormous, bony knuckles. He spoke in a piping tenor that verged on the falsetto.

"I mean to say, you've got your world, and I've got mine. It's your job to find things out, and it's mine to keep my fag-hole shut, isn't it?"

Kenworthy made room for Wright to put one elbow on the counter.

"What're you having?"

"I'll have a half of mild."

The man in the fur coat looked at Wright as if he did not exist.

"You bastards know bloody well I didn't do it, otherwise you'd have kept me inside, wouldn't you? It stands to sense, doesn't it? Once you've got your bloody knife into a family, they've had it, haven't they?"

The youth in the Moldavian hussar's uniform sniggered.

"I'll tell you what," Fur Coat said, "I wish I had have killed him, straight I do. If I get hold of the chap who did before you buggers do, I'll buy him a Scotch."

"Oh, Chick," the little girl said, "you hadn't ought to talk like that."

"Get knotted!"

Wright picked up his glass, bringing it up to his lips with extreme care, so as not to spill a drop on the precious fur.

"There'll be a bit more room in a few minutes," Kenworthy said, "they're all going to a dance."

Chick knocked back a fluid ounce of neat spirit in a gesture of magnificence.

"Cripes, it's hot in here!" he said, and began to take off the fur, his neighbours scrumming together to create the necessary space for him to do so. To Wright's surprise, he was wearing beneath the coat not merely a leather jerkin, but also a roll-necked woollen sweater. He looked down at the little girl.

"What are you drinking, Putty?"

Wright did not catch her reply, but the tattered matron behind the bar leaned forward in self-defence.

"Here! How old are you? You've no right to be in here."

Chick slapped the counter with the flat of his hand.

"She's eighteen today," he said, and those within earshot began to chant unmusically.

> *Happy birthday to you,*
> *Happy birthday to you,*
> *Happy birthday, dear Putty,*
> *Happy birthday to you.*

When the singing had died down, Kenworthy touched her gently on the fore-arm.

"What would you like, my dear?"

"I'd like a cherry brandy."

Kenworthy nodded reassuringly across the bar.

"It's on me, landlady."

Chick rolled his eyes towards the ceiling.

"Cripes! Drinking with the bloody bogies!"

The girl picked up the glass and looked at the play of light through the liqueur. Wright thought that Kenworthy was taking a dangerous chance. For all her soft voice and liquid eyes, she was as common as gutter-scrapings, and she was nowhere near eighteen.

Chick moved suddenly, so that he caught her with his elbow, and a few drops of the drink were splashed over her lapel.

"You can drink with cops, or you can come dancing with me," he said, picking up his fur and fumbling with the sleeve. All round the bar glasses were raised and drained.

"Oh, Chick!"

Kenworthy looked at her benevolently.

"Don't let me influence you," he said. "I'm prepared to

buy you an illicit drink, but one's the limit, and my dancing days are done. I will, at least, see you home."

The girl looked uneasily at Chick.

"You've had it," he said. "You had it the moment you took that drink off him. Now butter him up! I should worry! Every word he pumps out of you will help to put me in the bloody clear."

He swathed himself in the coat and turned his back on the bar. The coarse-featured blonde seized his right arm. The amateur hussar took a half step backwards. The gang stood up from their tables.

"Right!" Chick said. "Let's go and break up the bloody dance-hall!"

His friends made a gangway for him, and he led them jostling into the night. Putty was crying quietly, the tears grooving channels into her cheap cosmetics.

"I'm sorry about that," Kenworthy said, "but you could do better than him, you know. One day, I hope you will."

"You've all got Chick wrong. That's what's making him worse than he is."

Kenworthy passed her the handkerchief from his breast pocket, and she dabbed the corners of her eyes.

"Nevertheless, he did announce just now, to a collection of sputniks and satellites who look ready for anything, that he's about to break up a dance-hall."

"He won't," she said. "He's always saying things. He never does them. He can't dance—that's why he has it in for dance-halls."

"He *never* does things? There's a dossier back at the police-station that wouldn't exactly win him a Sunday School prize—"

"Oh—that—"

Putty dismissed with a sweep of her arm the record of breaking and entering, petty shop-lifting and larceny.

"Oh—that—. He's just plumb stupid, Chick is—just *stupid*."

The matter-of-fact emphasis which she gave to the word showed that she had settled down emotionally. She picked up her glass and sipped at her drink with rather absent-minded relish.

"It was nice of you to buy me this. I suppose you'll want me to answer a lot of questions, now."

"You can talk to me if you like. I'm not going to interrogate you, if that's what you're afraid of. As Chick said, nothing you say is likely to do him any harm. I don't want to harp on the theme—but after all, I am in Fellaby for only one purpose.—Take your time with your drink, girl. We can talk on the way home.—Have you had anything to eat, Shiner?"

"Not yet, sir."

"Order some sandwiches for the pair of us, for when I get back to the hotel. I don't expect I shall be late."

Wright finished his sour beer and walked back along the High Street. His greatest fear was that Kenworthy would close the case single-handed.

• 3 •

WRIGHT BOUGHT A bottle of light ale, mainly in order to give himself something to do, and sat in the County's select mezzanine bar, idly turning the sheets of his evening paper. Now and then, snippets of conversation drifted to him from a group who had just emerged from a meeting in a private room.

"It's all settled, then. We take them by surprise, and put Durkin into an alderman's seat. He'll be flattered into accepting, despite his party line."

The speaker was the obvious leader, a tall, well preserved, elderly man, with a flawless white carnation in his button-hole and a complexion so florid that he would have been written off as a caricature in a waxworks.

"So there'll be an unexpected vacancy in South West, and that's where we put Loombe in."

This came from a smaller, rather younger man, largely bald, and of conventionally military appearance. The florid character turned suddenly, as if he had known for the last two minutes that Wright was eaves-dropping, and thrust his chin within an inch or two of the sergeant's face.

"Oh, hullo—you one of the fellows they've brought up from Scotland Yard? Well, get it settled for us without any messing about, there's a good lad. Nasty business. Bloody nasty business. I liked Ted Barson. We all did. One of the best up-and-coming strengths we've had since the war. Damned shame about his wife and family. Lovely family. Don't forget—anything you want to know about who's who in Fellaby, any time, night or day—I keep open house."

He did not say who he was, presumably because he

moved through life without ever experiencing any such necessity. When the party had broken up, Wright asked the barman.

"That? Sir Howard Lesueur. Owns the Hall and about two hundred acres over on Fellaby Moor. Divisional chairman of the party. Doesn't take part in council affairs himself, wouldn't have time, but always busy with something or other—hospital management, old folks' welfare, and all that. Real old-fashioned gentleman, sir."

"And his friends?"

"All conservative councillors, sir—except Bill Hawley, Colonel Hawley, Sir Howard's agent.—Well, he's a bit of everything, really: agent for the estate, political agent for the constituency—do anything for anybody. He's been a friend to a lot of people in Fellaby, has Bill Hawley. Wonderful war record, too. Were you wanting anything else, sir? Only I'm waiting to close. Of course, if you want anything later on, you've only to ask the night porter, you being a resident, see? I always leave a crate out for him, in case—"

Wright sat alone in the deserted bar. It was a quarter to midnight when Kenworthy came in, his cheeks reddened by the chill of the evening and an impudent light in his eyes that comported paradoxically with his close-cropped grey hair and sparse, middle-aged frame.

"Sorry, Shiner. Been courting—"

"They come younger every year, sir—"

"Fifteen and a half," Kenworthy said.

"That staggers me. I knew she was young—"

". . . And she's drunk more cherry brandy in the last six months than you've had in your life-time.—A nice girl, other things being equal—the sort of child I wouldn't mind having for my own daughter.—Oh, don't get me wrong, Shiner—I'd have made something a damned sight different of her than what she is. I hope.—And she's just taken me the length of Fellaby's traditional courting-walk.—Did you do anything about those sandwiches?"

Wright rang for the porter. Kenworthy grinned.

"Not the ideal night for romance, Shiner—with a thin drizzle that had pretty well soaked my shirt before I remembered to turn my coat collar up. We started off by the gas-works. And here's a bit of local knowledge, Shiner, if ever you need it—if you start a courting walk by Fellaby gas-works, you take Park Street if the wind's in the east, and St. Barnabas Road if it's in the west. That way, you've always got the stink to lee-ward, see? Well, after the gas-works, we went up Coalpit Lane. Doesn't exactly sound like a nature reserve, does it? When you see it, you'll know what gets into poets when they talk about the last lamp, and all that twaddle. Fair pissing down by now, it was, but we were arm in arm by this time—no point in doing things by halves—so we couldn't care less."

The sandwiches arrived.

"I didn't know whether you'd want white or brown, so I ordered half and half. And half chicken, half ham."

Kenworthy appeared to pay no attention. He picked up a segment of tomato from the garnishing and popped it in his mouth.

"After that, she took me down the tow-path. No inhibitions about that lass. Showed me where it happened. And I'll tell you what, Shiner—he couldn't have chosen a better spot for it. Dead ground to the sky-line in every direction, and a get-away over waste land in at least three different directions, if someone had surprised him. Then she showed me the ruin, the gang's HQ, Wardle's, they call it. That's where Chick found the Luger, the morning after. He often looks in at HQ on his way to work—when he goes to work. So he found the gun, and had the good sense to pick it up in his handkerchief, otherwise I don't suppose they'd have bothered to call you and me up here. Then he hid it away again, intending to pick it up at the end of the day and hang on to it for his own purposes. That, of course, would have made him look no end of a lad in the eyes of his crew, but Putty managed to persuade him it was bloody daft. In any case, when he went again in the evening, our lot had been in and nicked it. So the question remains purely academic."

Kenworthy helped himself to a chicken sandwich.

"Anyway, she let me take her home after that. At least, we said good-night among the dust-bins, far enough from the house for her father not to come out and give me a belting for having her out so late. Shiner—I think she has a bit of a crush on me."

"I'm not surprised," Wright said.

"Green eyes, Shiner?—I never knew you cared!—At any rate, I've heard enough about Chick to eliminate him once and for all. Odd doubts will keep cropping up from time to time, and you'll see the local boys getting restless about him. So if ever we want them off our shoulders for a half a day or so, we can let them plod on. But Chick doesn't worry me. He's just dead phoney. Everything about him belongs to his brother, anyway—even the fur coat and leadership of the gang. And I gather that isn't scheduled to last much longer. Do you know what, Shiner?"

Kenworthy twisted a sprig of parsley with his thumb.

"I don't know what sort of damned clobber aldermen wear when they're on duty—but that fur coat means as much to Chick as Barson's ermine, or whatever it is, meant to him. And for precisely the same reason—a sign that you came from the wrong side of the tracks, but you've risen above it, you'd like to think. Now we've got to find out how Barson hauled himself over the embankment."

Wright retailed the remarks he had heard from the political whisper-shapers.

"The alderman is dead, long live the alderman!" Kenworthy said. "I've been shaken two or three times tonight. Take Putty, for example. She doesn't know the first thing about local government. Ignorant as hell. Wouldn't know a town clerk from a newt's bum. And, of course, she hates Barson's side like poison. Her idea of reverence for the dead is to refer to the late lamented as a 'fat, stuck-up pig.' But at the back of all that there's a sort of faith that I couldn't eradicate. Our darling little Putty is a materialist, an iconoclast, a dispeller of fancy dreams about Lugers and fur coats—but she still has a lingering sort of belief that aldermen mean something in this world, that they are possessed of some god-awful power, that they are in some way capable of shaping human destiny. Pathetic, isn't it?"

He pushed the rest of the sandwiches towards Wright and stood up to go to bed.

"Here. Finish these. Part of the duties of a sergeant on assignment—eating up the super's leavings."

"There is just one small point, sir."

"I hope it *is* a small one."

"I went down to the museum, sir."

"Oh, yes?"

"Well, sir—I don't know whether you've ever broken a window and pulled the remainder of the glass fragments out—"

"Infrequently."

"Would you pull the bits towards you, or ease them away from you?"

"I'm sure I don't know what an expert witness would say."

"I'll swear that most men would pull them towards them—especially if they were trying to be as quiet as they could."

"You may be right."

"Well—nearly all the glass at the museum—and certainly all the larger pieces—were found on the outside of the window. But it was perfectly apparent that they had been pulled inwards from the inside. I examined the framework very carefully, and all the putty—"

"There's that word again!"

Wright struggled to control himself.

"It was you who sent me to the museum, sir!"

"Sorry, Shiner."

"All the putty had been compressed towards the inside and splayed out on the outside."

"You're suggesting?"

"That the museum wasn't broken into at all. That evidence suggesting a break-in was faked."

"An interesting thought, Shiner. Might be far-fetched, but you could be right. Might be worth remembering, before we've finished. Anyway, good-night for now."

He turned his back and went down the corridor towards his bedroom. He did not look as if the new theory had made any impact at all. Wright went up the few steps to his own corridor, found his own bedroom, where he lay fitfully awake throughout the smaller hours. He woke again at five, and again at six. He was already sitting at a table when Kenworthy came down to breakfast, but had forborne to order anything until the superintendent joined him.

The morning papers had made joyful play about the man

in the Robin Hood hat. Kenworthy folded his *Daily Mail* to the back page and propped it against the tea-pot.

"I see United have dropped Forbes for Saturday."

"I see the Identikit picture's on the front page."

"Shiner—do you know what happens to policemen who never take their minds off their work?"

Wright breakfasted modestly, Kenworthy hugely, following up all the by-ways of the menu.

"Always breakfast well in a hotel, Shiner—even if only because the taxpayer has to pay for it, whether you eat it or not. Well—I suppose we might as well get over to the Report Centre. There's the daily conference at nine, and something fresh might have come in overnight."

There was a first interim report on Barson's army service.

"I see he had V.D.," Wright said. "I suppose we shouldn't judge him too harshly for that, considering the morals of the time and place. Thousands of others did."

"And thousands didn't. I didn't, for one."

"And this is interesting, sir. He seems to have been under close arrest for a fortnight, pending a court martial that never materialised. Large scale black market. Flogging army stores. He and half a dozen others from his unit, including an officer. But the S.I.B. jumped the gun. So anxious to get a case that they muffed the evidence. The whole thing fell through on a technicality."

Kenworthy held out his hand for the typescript.

"This could be it, Shiner. Blackmailed or blackmailing. We shall have to get the Yard on to this. Speak to inspector Heather—and don't let him pull any fast ones about manpower shortage. We need to know who Barson's associates were at the time, what's become of them since, whether any of them have made any journeys recently—"

"Such as Robin Hood?"

Kenworthy assumed an expression calculated to damp juvenile enthusiasms.

"Let's not wear blinkers, Shiner. There remain other possibilities. Just get on to Heather, and if he tries to offer you short commons, tell him I'll be ringing him later."

Then superintendent Rhys came in, uniformed men stood self-consciously to attention at their filing trays and telephones, and in a flurry of sharpened pencils and ready note-books, the conference began.

Wright sat in silent admiration for the way in which, without a note in front of him, Kenworthy presented a situation report and appreciation of the case. In crisp, quiet, unspeculative tones he expounded fact after fact, detail after detail, eschewing all irrelevance, listing working theories, and showing emotional preference for none of them. What a hell of a classifying brain the man had!

"We must also bear in mind the possibility that the burglary at the museum may itself have been faked. The window could have been broken from the inside, and the thief might have made his entry in some much more comfortable way. This is a piece of intelligent speculation on the part of sergeant Wright, and there may be evidence to support it. We cannot speak with greater certainty at present."

But he said not a word about Putty.

"And today's priority, superintendent?"

"The man in the green felt hat. Whatever background information London can give us, it still remains important to pick up all the gen in this locality. Further house-to-house enquiry, including districts well away from the Carlton estate, and I don't care how many thousand more question-naires it runs to. We want to know all we can about this man. Particularly, what sort of news about Barson inter-ested him. What titbits about Barson's habits made him prick up his ears? What sort of suggestions about Barson's way of life did he use as a prompter? Even when we get hold of the man himself, it may be something in one of the questionnaires that will finally nail him. So have a second go, even, at those who've already come forward with something.—You've put on one side those questionnaires with a positive showing?"

In a matter of seconds, a constable produced a thin wad of these.

"And how many of these are in Carlton Avenue?"

"More than half, sir."

"Were there any residents in Carlton Avenue who came up with nothing at all about Green Hat?"

"Very few, sir."

"Let me see their questionnaires."

He turned to Wright.

"We'll do Carlton Avenue ourselves, this morning. We mustn't be dilatory about calling on Barson's widow, and we can take in other households at the same time."

The clerical officer came up smartly with the requested papers.

"Only two, in fact, sir."

"And they do not mention Green Hat at all?"

"Not at all, sir."

"Good! They'll be a good start."

• 4 •

CARLTON AVENUE SWEPT down to the canal, from which it was screened by a row of maturing poplars. It was entirely post-war in building, and was, one could see at first sight, an expensive estate.

"If you'll notice," Kenworthy said, "the people round here have their pelmets on the outside of their curtains. That's because they furnish their homes for the sake of their neighbours, instead of for themselves. In most cases this is the first generation that hasn't lived in Coronation Street."

They passed a garden full of little gnomes and ornamental foot-bridges.

"It's common courtesy to call on Mrs. Barson first. Let's get it over with."

The Barsons' house was a detached, double fronted villa set well back behind an open forecourt garden in which every corner had been laid with geometrical precision. An imitation well, with windlass and red oaken bucket, took pride of place. Kenworthy looked down at the faultless paving-stones of the drive and side-paths.

"Costs a small fortune before you even wipe your feet."

Inside the front door a wrought iron Mexican pushed a large barrow bearing all manner of cacti. The tendrils of a pale green climbing plant spread over the wall. A row of hanging tiles depicted a series of vintage motor cars. An indigo Tretchikoff in a contemporary frame beamed vitality over the household. They caught sight of a Colson dishwasher on the kitchen draining-board.

Barson's widow was a very small, trim woman in her early thirties, with immaculately set straw blonde hair and a somewhat thin-featured prettiness that showed even through her evident grief.

"I'm sure that I need not say—"

Kenworthy's voice was no more than a whisper in his throat.

"I need not say how reluctant we are to disturb you."

"I realise you have a duty to do. And if I can tell you anything that might help you—"

She spoke in a shallow, distant voice, not unmarked by traces of the local accent, but in no way cheapened by it. She had probably played a very retiring part on the fringe of her husband's public life.

"Local officers will already have asked you whether your husband had any enemies—"

"He used to fight people politically, but it would be wrong to call them enemies. I always thought they enjoyed it, really, under the surface. It always made me feel a little sick. But certainly there was no one who would—would have hurt him. Sometimes they even had a drink together after the most bitter committee meetings. It never seemed to me to make sense."

"We're interested in this man who was asking questions about him from house to house. But of course, he wouldn't have come here—"

"Oh—but he did."

She went to the mantelpiece, and from a letter-rack brought out a religious pamphlet, decorated with the silhouette of a pair of lovers in the shadow of an oblique cross.

"We get these people down here from time to time—Mormons and Jehovah's Witnesses, and that kind of thing. I never encourage them."

"But this one was a bit more persistent than most, was he? A bit nosy—trying to get a good look round while you had the door open?"

"He said he thought he knew Edward. He said he had served in the same army unit, but in a different company, so Edward wouldn't remember him."

"You told your husband about this?"

"I mentioned it."

"Did it interest him?"

"No. He just brushed it off. He said he didn't know the

man, but that there must be hundreds who knew him. We didn't talk about it any more."

"Tell me, Mrs. Barson—was your husband at all keen on keeping up his former army contacts? Did he go to regimental reunions, or anything like that?"

"No. He always said there was no point in living in the past. He went to a British Legion dinner once a year, but that was usually in an official capacity."

Kenworthy looked with a sudden jerk at the radiogram— the last and most expensive word in stereophonic equipment.

"Fond of music, Mrs. Barson?"

"I love it. So did Edward. Not this modern stuff. We like Mantovani, and *Friday Night is Music Night*."

Kenworthy settled back in his chair.

"I'm sorry, Mrs. Barson. There are just one or two other little questions, and then we'll leave you to yourself.—You knew your husband during his army days, but you were not married till afterwards—is that right?"

"Yes. We wrote to each other, but we were not engaged until his twenty-first birthday."

"And he was a corporal?"

"That's right."

"Did he write often?"

"Well—you know what men are. Sometimes it would go three weeks or a month. But I don't see—"

"Did he tell you a lot about his army life?"

"Not a great deal. He liked Germany, and sent some lovely descriptions. Superintendent—do you really think that what's happened goes back to those days?"

"Do you?" he asked, with sudden harshness.

She was too surprised to answer. He softened his tone at once, but offered no apology.

"We'd better get a description of this man who called, just to make sure it tallies. Then we've done."

But she had evidently read her morning newspaper, for involuntarily she spoke only in its phraseology. Nevertheless, Wright recorded punctiliously all she said, and then they took their leave.

"Right!" Kenworthy said, looking at his notebook. "Mrs. Crispin, *Mine-an-ers*. Wonder where the hell that is?

They wouldn't have anything as plebeian as house-numbers, would they?"

The house was a smaller, less opulent, but nevertheless expensively regimented home on the opposite side of the avenue. There was no imitation well in the garden, but bulbs were beginning to sprout in a diminutive green and yellow wheelbarrow. The Mexican inside the door was smaller than Barson's, and his less intricate handcart carried fewer succulents. The tiles on the wall depicted a series of fair-ground traction-engines, and instead of a Tretchikoff there was a cubist group of red and blue horses.

Mrs. Crispin was a chubby woman in her early twenties, with impudently up-tilted nose and buttocks swelling out of her royal blue slacks.

"I told the other officers—there's nothing I can tell you."

"We're simply interested in the man who came with religious tracts."

"He didn't come here."

"Mind if we come in?"

Kenworthy was well into the house before she could protest. Wright followed. In the front room, cups, side-plates, bowls of brown sugar and plates of fancy biscuits were laid on a multitude of side-tables.

"We're having an Oxfam coffee morning at eleven. I hope this isn't going to take long."

"That's up to you."

Kenworthy picked up a folded letter from the mantel-piece.

"You've got a nerve," she said.

"Nothing to the nerve I'll have if I come back here with a search warrant."

He put back the letter.

"What's your husband do for a living, Mrs. Crispin?"

"He's a company director."

"That tells me nothing."

"Wait till he comes home. Then you can ask him."

"About this door-to-door evangelist—"

"How many more times?—He didn't call at every house in the avenue."

"There are five of your neighbours prepared to swear on oath that he called at this one—"

He looked at his watch.

"—and in ten minutes they'll be here contributing to world famine.—What did he do?—Take you up for a tumble on the bed?"

She was speechless.

"Doesn't worry *me*," Kenworthy said. "That type takes it where he can find it. And I expect you get a bit tired of *mine-an-ers* from time to time. It's all right, Mrs. Crispin—there's no need for your husband to find out. Although he might get a little inquisitive, if I have to take you in for questioning."

"What do you want to know?" she asked.

"Well, it strikes me that in exchange for favours received, he'd want to know a lot more than most of your neighbours would have told him—about alderman Edward Barson."

"He asked me an awful lot of questions. I couldn't tell him much."

It was heavy going. She had seen no significant pattern in Green Hat's inquisition, and her memory was woolly. Wright knew intuitively when Kenworthy expected him to join in the prompting.

Had Barson held many private committee meetings at his house? Did he entertain a lot? What sort of people came to see him? Were they local big-wigs, or were there often strangers from outside the town? He had a pretty expensive home, hadn't he? Was he always taking delivery of something new? Was it all on hire purchase? Did H.P. collectors often call on the Barsons? Did Mrs. Barson sometimes pretend she was out when she wasn't?

"And did she?" Kenworthy asked.

"How should I know?"

"No. I should think you were too busy keeping out of sight yourself, if that sort of laddie was in the road."

"You ought to try keeping house on ten quid a week."

"I've lived on less in my time."

"There was one thing that interested him specially. He wouldn't leave it alone.—Mrs. Barson's garden."

"What about it?"

"He wanted to know whether Mr. Barson did it himself.

Who mowed the lawn? Who did the autumn digging? Who made the well?"

"Who did?"

"The men from the Parks Department.—Oh, there's nothing wrong in that. They'll contract to do your garden for you, provided it doesn't interfere with their official work. Only it's terribly expensive. And, of course, there's a waiting list. We wouldn't stand an earthly chance, even if we could afford it. But with Mr. Barson being an alderman—"

"The council workmen came to his garden regularly?"

"That's what this man wanted to know. And he kept on about the paving-stones on Mr. Barson's drive—which are the same as those on the pavements in the town—"

"I noticed that," Kenworthy said.

"Well, that's all above board. The council will do your drive for you, when their own work's slack. Several people in the avenue have had it done. But it's expensive. My husband worked out that it costs more than a private firm."

"The stones were delivered by corporation lorry, were they?"

"Of course. What would you expect them to use? Bakers' vans?"

"What time of day was this delivery made? Morning? Afternoon?"

"This man asked that, too. In the evening. I expect they were working overtime. That would be more expensive still, wouldn't it?"

"It might," Kenworthy said, and looked at the eight-day clock. It was already ten past eleven. There was no sign of her guests. Mrs. Crispin looked suddenly haggard.

"Don't worry," Kenworthy said. "They'll come. Wild horses wouldn't keep them away, now we've been. You'll see the corners of their curtains shifting delicately as the sergeant and I go up the road. And remember this, Mrs. Crispin—I don't want a word to leak to a soul about the turn this conversation's taken, or I'll have an article on your moral stamina headlined in the *Gazette*, the *Herald* and *Old Mother Shipton's Weekly*. Understand?"

He did not speak again until he and Wright were well away from the estate.

• 5 •

KENWORTHY FIXED AN appointment with the town clerk for two o'clock that afternoon.

"And for the rest of this morning, we'll find ourselves a cosy corner in the Public Library, and run through every available copy of the two local rags for the last ten years. I know this will have been done for us, and I seem to remember there was a digest on the file, but there's nothing like our own sweet eyes."

This involved another meeting with the curator of the museum, this time in his role as Borough Librarian. Gill still presented the same restless, obsequious figure which Wright had observed on the previous afternoon—not exactly hopping from foot to foot, not quite wringing his hands, but it would not have seemed out of character if he had begun to do either at any moment.

"I would gladly give you the use of my own office, gentlemen—but there's a lot of coming and going, besides the telephone. So—"

He took them to a long, narrow room which was used for bookbinding, cataloguing and pasting in labels. And he brought in personally, looking as if he would crack under their weight, enormous files of bound newspapers, those of the last few months still between cardboard covers.

"I'll see to it that you're not disturbed in here."

They settled down to scan the long, dated sheets, occasionally drawing each other's attention to some particular item. It soon became apparent that the *Gazette* and the *Herald* were poles apart in the aims and achievements of journalism. The *Herald*, smaller in format and circulation, went in for blatant sensationalism, often taking speakers' high-lights unashamedly out of context. The *Gazette*, on the other hand, was a family paper of stern reserve. Both publications proclaimed themselves independent.

It also became clear that Barson had been a consummate master of vituperation. He could work himself into a frenzy over a triviality and could pursue a hatred to the last ditch of reason. He would attack an opponent's scheme simply because the man was an opponent, and with total disregard for the merits of what was being put forward. At the same time, he was uninhibited by considerations of conscience or consistency. He felt, apparently, under no obligation to remember from week to week what he had said.

"If my name were Durkin," Wright remarked, "I certainly wouldn't be choking back my tears at the grave-side. Durkin seems to have been one of his favourite whipping-boys."

"Oh, I don't know. You'll find some of these people get a queer kick out of this kind of thing."

But it was not only politicians who fell foul of Barson's displeasure. Officials were often flailed, including juniors, who were in no position to hit back. One of his cultivated images had evidently been as a guardian of the public purse. He regularly opposed expenditure, sometimes on obvious essentials, and the county rate, particularly the cost of education, for which the borough had no responsibility, was an opportunity for his voluble wrath at frequent intervals.

"Look at this," Kenworthy said. "Three years ago there was a salary increase for local government clerical workers. A national award, properly negotiated, Whitley Council, and the whole creaking machine. He even had a go at that. Lord knows, he'd no chance there, and he must have known that as well as anyone else, but he couldn't keep his mouth shut."

"He must have been an embarrassment to his own side."

"Not necessarily so. Probably now and then they'd have a quiet word with him in a corner, to calm him down. But you've got to admit, Shiner, this stuff makes good reading. Fearless Barson! What's he said this week? It sells news-papers. It also sells votes. And, like it or not, there are voters who think and feel as Barson did. Vote for Barson, and let's put an end to all kinds of nonsense. What about lunch, Shiner? I'm famished."

Early in the afternoon they paid their call on the town clerk, an elderly, quiet, capable but tired man, who smiled readily, but seldom with his eyes. There were formal courtesies, and grave condolences over the shock that had smitten Fellaby. Then Kenworthy came bluntly to his point.

"Mr. Belfield—I want to know whether alderman Barson paid properly and officially for the work your Park gardeners did at his own home."

"Oh, I'm sure he did. It is by no means unusual, you know, although, of course, they can't do as much as people would wish. Our municipal claims on their time must be met first."

"Of course. And I don't really expect there to have been any fiddle. But I think that the matter is going to be raised before long in a quarter which neither you nor I can control."

"Quite so. Well—this is easily looked into. And I don't doubt the outcome of the enquiry."

"There's also the question of a delivery of paving-stones, sand and cement at Barson's home, one evening between April and June last year."

The town clerk looked troubled.

"The civic funeral tomorrow, and innuendoes of corruption today."

"And one of your aldermen who may have been shot dead by someone who was trying to blackmail him."

The town clerk took on fresh, brisk tones.

"Of course, gentlemen, if there's anything in the nature of a malpractice within this borough, there shall be no hesitation in ferreting it out. I'll bring in the Borough Engineer; this is his pigeon."

He spoke on the house telephone, and then there was desultory conversation about the architectural show-pieces of Fellaby until the Borough Engineer came in. The town clerk explained the nature of the suspicions in a couple of economical sentences, and the Engineer was away again, looking at the two detectives with covert curiosity. It was some time before he returned, and then it was with a file under his arm from which papers were spilling.

"The receipts for the gardeners' time and labour are all in order. The other matter doesn't seem to be quite so easy. I shall need a little more time. It may be necessary to have a word with the yard foreman."

Kenworthy nodded.

"We'll not waste any time over this," the town clerk said. "I'll telephone you the moment we've made sure."

When the Engineer had left them again, he stood up and went over to his window, which overlooked the wintry trees of the park.

"Probably the dockets have been misfiled, or something."

"In any case, the Borough Engineer will want to discuss it with you first, as the Borough's principal legal adviser."

The town clerk brought his fist into the palm of his hand.

"I must confess, gentlemen, I'm not very hopeful. And if Barson were alive, I can tell you, this moment would be bringing me little pain. As it is, what can come of it? Even more misery for Enid Barson. The high jump for one or three of our employees, who probably had little effective choice in the matter. And there you are, you see—I'm already prejudging the whole issue."

"You could tell us a lot about Barson," Kenworthy said.

"I could, I can and I will. In good time. At the moment I'm longing for you two to go out of that door so that I can have a tête-à-tête with my own Borough Engineer."

Kenworthy took his hat from the stand.

"Sergeant Wright—we have other fish to fry."

• 6 •

WHEN THEY LEFT the town hall, Kenworthy sent Wright back to the library, saying that he himself had better "sit and mess about with telephones and look scientific" for an hour or two.

Wright sat down in an atmosphere of ink, paste and buckram and continued to turn the pages of effete newsprint. At half-past three, the girl from the borrowing desk brought him a cup of tea and a few minutes later the nerve-racked Mr. Gill tapped the door and came in carrying his own cup.

"I hope I'm not interrupting."

He perched himself on a corner of one of the workbenches.

"No. Glad of a break, to tell you the truth. This study gets a bit wearisome."

"I trust you're finding what you're looking for."

Wright looked down at his wad of accumulated notes.

"Yes, sir. Three bags full. With all due reverence, the late departed was no introvert."

Gill smiled pathetically.

"I could tell you a thing or two."

"Yes. You certainly don't seem to have escaped his attentions."

Gill slid his diminutive back-side off the bench and picked up one of the bound volumes.

"Look at this!"

Barson had moved that Gill's salary be reduced by five pounds a year, "as a token, marking our dissatisfaction at

the sub-standard services provided." The motion had not
found a seconder.

"I was at fault there," Gill said. "I suppose any admin-
istrator can trip up over a detail now and then. A technical
college student had asked for some particularly recondite
volume to be borrowed from the central library, and one of
my assistants had overlooked it.—Not, mind you, that I am
trying to shelter behind a subordinate; a responsible officer
must be prepared to answer for the weaknesses in his
department.—At any rate, the student mentioned it in the
hearing of alderman Barson, and this was the outcome."

"I'm sure there'd be plenty of people to support you in
such a situation," Wright said.

"Oh, yes—and it was well known that I was always one
of Barson's number one targets. The thing had become
almost a standing joke—with everyone but me—"

"Yes. I remember one or two instances," Wright said,
and tapped his notes with a pencil. "Obscene books in the
art section—"

"There was a photograph of a nude in the standard
album. I'll guarantee you'll find it in every branch library of
this size in the country."

"Communist propaganda in the Reading Room—"

"We'd taken the *Daily Worker* for years—since long
before my appointment. I always strive to represent all
shades of political opinion."

"But you found yourself branded a red."

Gill smiled.

"It didn't seem funny at the time. But there's a difference
between the argy-bargy of local government and shooting
down a defenceless man.—Well, you mustn't let me hold
you up.—If at any time I can help in any way—"

Gill left him, and Wright pressed on through the folios
until the print began to make him dizzy. He went back to the
hotel and found Kenworthy impatiently waiting to go in for
the evening meal.

"I've got a job for you tonight, Shiner, and God knows
how you're going to do it, but I want every scrap of
information you can squeeze out of the situation. The
diversional labour party are meeting here tonight, to draw

up their own plan of campaign. I want to know what's said. Any idea how you'll set about it?"

"Not yet."

"Good! Neither would I have. Well, let's have an early supper. I've got a date with Putty, and I don't want to let her down."

As they ate, Kenworthy let fall bits of news that had come in through the Report Centre. They had unearthed, for example, the former Military Police sergeant of the Special Investigation Branch, who had so nearly brought Barson to early retribution. He was now an inspector in a borough force in a neighbouring county, and would be coming over the next day to give a first-hand account of the affair in Westphalia.

"Inspector Heather's done a first-rate job of work there, Shiner. He's dug out the whereabouts of all those six who were charged alongside Barson, their post-war goings-on, and everything. A bright bunch they are, too. Only one's been inside, and he seems to have settled down comfortably since. Of course, they got away with a king's ransom in that original piece of villainy, if only they found some means of salting it away, which shouldn't have been too difficult. One of them owns a big garage, another's a solicitor's managing clerk. The lieutenant in the case has stood for parliament— unsuccessfully—and sits on the boards of at least half a dozen quite respectable companies."

"Any of them likely to have been hereabouts recently?"

"That remains to be gone into. Heather's on the ball. But we mustn't assume that it's only those directly connected with the army crime who might be of interest. Any man in the unit who knew what was going on might have seen its future possibilities. Heather's got quite a lot of spade-work in front of him still. And I was hoping that Malpas would have come up with his report on *Futurco Publicity* by now. Damn it, it was only half a day's work, and Bradcaster isn't the end of the world. We've got quite a day ahead of us tomorrow. And the rank and file are working like Trojans on the questionnaire. County are feeding the stuff experimentally into a computer. There's no telling what that'll serve up."

Kenworthy screwed up his paper table-napkin and declined coffee.

"At eighteenpence a thimbleful, it isn't worth it," he said. "Besides, I think Putty knows a caff where we can get a reasonable beaker for sevenpence."

"I wish you wouldn't call her by that ridiculous name," Wright said.

"Putty? Short for Patricia. Best she could make of it when she was in the teething-ring and rattle stage. Makes her sound sort of innocent, don't you think? By the way, did you happen to notice which way the wind was blowing?"

"I did not."

"A young detective should notice everything. So should an old one. It makes a lot of difference, which way you pass the gasworks."

Wright was left to the by now familiar delights of the County Hotel. By dint of making one small bottle of beer last a very long time, he managed to watch the left wing party arrive in their twos and threes and take possession of the same small room that Sir Howard and his group had used. Their faces had tougher lines, mostly, than those of their political rivals, though there were one or two who appeared at once to be the intellectuals of the team.

A bell called the barman for orders, and he returned to them with a tray of drinks. When he came back, he collected Wright's empty bottle as an excuse to whisper in his ear.

"Would you believe it? They've just stood for a minute's silence for Barson."

"I'm surprised that they have their meetings here. Haven't they got their own headquarters in the town?"

"Oh—this isn't an official meeting. This is an under-the-counter pressure group—the anti-Durkin faction. Besides—they like coming here. If you ask me, the only reason they want to get into power is so that they can play at being Tories."

"You don't seem to have much room for either side."

"I haven't, sir. I've seen too much of both of them. To tell you the truth, I don't use my vote at all. I never go. I reckon it's all a waste of time."

Wright transferred his empty glass to the counter for the

sake of continuing the conversation whenever it was free of
other customers, but although the bar was not unduly
crowded, there was sufficient coming and going of small
groups to prevent much progress. He found himself button-
holed by the editor of the *Herald*, a back-slapping little
extrovert called Manterfield, who did his best to tease from
him some remark that could be twisted into a brassy
headline, but he was saved from elaborate prevarication by
chief inspector Dunne, Grayling's burly second-in-command,
who beckoned Wright into a corner. He was in a mood that
seemed strangely different from the jovial figure he had cut on
the previous night.

"Where's Kenworthy?"

"Out on enquiries."

"Did he say when he'd be back?"

"No. Latish, I expect."

"Something serious has come up. This fellow in the
green hat. The day Barson was killed, he spent the whole
afternoon in the Public Library."

"That's an easy one. He was probably doing what
Kenworthy and I did today—running over back numbers of
the *Gazette* and *Herald*."

"Would he have to spend three hours closeted with Gill
for that? With staff told not to knock, and telephone-calls
diverted to an extension?"

"Certainly not. Gill made excuses for Kenworthy and me
not to use his room."

"And he's had ample opportunity to come and talk to us.
He knows the furore that's on. Not only must the man have
something to hide, he must be more than a bit of a fool. He
must have known he couldn't keep this dark. It was one of
the girls from the lending-desk who came in with it. She
said she'd been sweating cobs all day, especially when you
were in there, wondering whether she ought to come
forward or not."

"Looks far-reaching," Wright said. "Gill had no reason
to love Barson. He talks openly about it."

"Looks as if this might be the key to the whole chute,
boy. The thing is—will Kenworthy want us to whip him
in?"

"I'm quite sure Kenworthy will want to handle this in his own way."

"Have you no way of getting in touch with him?"

Wright pictured Kenworthy chatting to Putty in a cobbled alley between two rows of slums, secure from the public gaze in the shadow behind some one's lavatory.

"No. He's essentially mobile."

"What's he on? Do you know? Fellaby isn't exactly a metropolis. I reckon I could soon put my hand on him."

"I doubt whether he'd appreciate that. I fancy he's working on a somewhat sensitive informant."

Wright looked at the clock. It was scarcely half past nine. On last night's form, it would be well over two hours before Kenworthy turned up. Dunne persisted.

"What sort of informant? Where did he pick him up, do you know?"

"He doesn't tell me everything. One of these teenage malcontents, I think."

"You're being bloody cagey, sergeant. I'm not working for a rival firm, you know."

"You'd be bloody cagey, chief inspector, if you had to work with Kenworthy—and live with him afterwards. If we upset him while he's in the middle of something that's just beginning to go the right way—"

Meanwhile, the pressure group had come out of committee, and were sprawling along the bar. Wright looked quickly in their direction. Dunne followed his glance irritably.

"Well, I'm for hauling Gill into the nick, sergeant."

"Knowing Kenworthy, I'm sure he'd prefer to deal with the man on his own ground."

"And if the bird's flown, he can always lean back and blame his country cousins."

"No need for the bird to fly," Wright said. "We can easily make sure he's still there. I'll ring up on some pretext—I can pull a wrong number act, if he answers himself. Then a plain-clothes man can watch the premises until Kenworthy comes back."

Dunne accepted this enthusiastically. His main concern was to be relieved of responsibility for the decision.

"Excellent idea, sergeant. And as I happen to know a

plain-clothes man who's got nothing better to do at the moment than sit here guzzling beer—"

Wright inclined his head towards the group at the bar.

"I'm supposed to be pumping that lot."

"Pumping that lot? You'd have those buggers dry in a couple of jerks. If there's anything you want to know about that lot, mate, you just ask me for half an hour of my time—"

So Wright left a note for Kenworthy and went out into the night. Even more satisfying than the wrong number routine was the fact that he heard Gill's voice without pressing Button A, and so was able to get his pennies back. He made his way to the grounds of the library, walking on the grass verges to avoid crunching the gravel, and remaining in the shadow of trees and shrubs as much as he could.

He worked his way behind rhododendrons to a point from which he could see two lighted windows on the top floor. Even at a distance of seventy yards he could hear music—a Beethoven trio, though he did not recognise it as such. In the room in which it was being played, it must have been inordinately loud; presumably Gill was a hi-fi enthusiast.

The trio came to an end, and there was a pause whilst the record was changed; the *Appassionata*, at a volume which no piano could have achieved. Wright stood through the whole of the sonata, his fingers numb with cold, and the tips of his ears barely tolerable. Then the music stopped. A light appeared behind the frosted window of a lavatory, and presently he heard the sound of flushing. The light was switched off, and so was that of the room in which the gramophone had been playing. Another light appeared, followed by the rush of water through down-flow pipes.

"Has he gone to bed?"

Wright started. Kenworthy was standing half a yard behind him.

"He's on his way."

"What are you messing about here for, then?"

"Chief inspector Dunne told me—"

"You take your orders from me, not from chief inspector Dunne."

"I know, but—"

"But nothing."

Kenworthy nodded towards Gill's flat.

"He's going nowhere tonight. We'll let him get well into his beauty sleep before we disturb him. Then we can put on our best Gestapo manners and clobber on his door in the middle of the night. Catch him at his lowest ebb. Get his statement while he's still blinking into our oil-lamps. Let's go and see what sort of brew they've got on in the nick."

Dunne was duty officer for the night, and had reverted to his characteristic high spirits now that Kenworthy had reappeared in charge. He received them in an office that was a miniature—but much less tidy—of Grayling's, and had tea brought in a variety of mugs and cups of which no two specimens were alike.

"What do you make of Gill?" Kenworthy asked him.

"Weedy so-and-so. Well—you've met him, haven't you? Scared of his own date-stamp—"

The chief inspector put on mincing tones.

"Well, Mr. Dunne, I'm afraid I'm going to have to dun you two-pence for that one, ha, ha, ha! Runs a decent library, I suppose. Too damned decent. But he usually has a dirty book under the counter for me and the chief super. At least, they're dirty to Gill's way of thinking. Last one he lent me was about a nest of homosexual postmen—but it never really got down to brass tacks. Left too much to the imagination, from which I don't suffer.—No—I hardly think of Gill advancing up the High Street, fanning his hammers."

Kenworthy picked up a match-end and parted the scum that was floating on top of his tea.

"I was going to drop in and see you before I turned in, anyway. Your uniformed branch is going to need a few reinforcements tomorrow night, from what I hear."

"Oh?"

"Yes. Matters have come to a head in the Stanway gang. It seems there are at least two candidates to take it over. Do the names Riley and Webbe mean anything to you?"

"I know Riley. Did him for receiving a raincoat last November. The other one's a new one on me."

"Thomas Webbe," Kenworthy said, "an outsider. Lives in Dalton Fell. Meets his O Group at a transport café in the Weeldon Road."

"I know it.—Sal's."

"That's right. Well—Webbe fancies his chances, and the showdown is tomorrow night. All three parties are canvassing for support among the villagers, so there might be quite a few characters in town. Stanway will operate from the *Saracen's Head*, Riley from the *Coconut Club*, Webbe from a mobile column."

Dunne made rapid notes on a pad.

"Thanks for the tip-off. Could be ugly."

"Tell me more about Stanway," Kenworthy said. "I don't attach much more importance to him, but we can't rule him out altogether. He might have had a brain-storm."

"If Chick had a brain-storm, it wouldn't wet the pavement. I could waft him across the road with my cap."

"What about his women-folk? I suppose he has a few camp-followers?"

"Several. There are one or two mad-brained enough to hang after him. Steady favourite is a little bint from up Hagley Brow. Putty, they call her. Putty Pearson. Dead rough. Well—her old man's been known to beat her mother up to procure a miscarriage, so you can tell."

"Does she—Putty Pearson—exert much influence over Chick?"

"I expect he reacts in the normal masculine way to the usual bits and pieces."

Dunne guffawed happily.

"I daresay it's his coat she's after."

The hands of the huge, institutional clock stood at midnight. Wright uncrossed and recrossed his legs. Kenworthy looked at him patronisingly. At a quarter to one they had another cup of tea. At twenty to two, Kenworthy started the *Evening News* crossword. At two o'clock he announced that they might perhaps think of moving.

"Not, mind you, that I think this is necessarily going to seal things off for us. It's rather like getting out of a maze by keeping your right hand on the wall. You get out in the end, but you have to go round all the blind alleys first."

• 7 •

CROSSING THE DESERTED town, Kenworthy reverted to what Wright was beginning to hope was his normal self—a mood in which he treated the sergeant as a reasonable being and an intelligent collaborator.

"Actually—I got a good deal out of Putty tonight."

"I should think, after the machinery you've just put into operation, you're just about washed up with Putty, as far as future dates are concerned."

"On the contrary, Shiner—Putty is a very anxious little girl. She wants nothing more than to see Chick eased out of his present mode of existence. The main thing is to see that he doesn't get hurt in the process. Of course, there'll be a pretty horrible time while she's trying to nurse his purely neurotic wounds. But she wants him out of the gang, and she feels she can help him over his fallen pride. But when I said I'd learned a lot, I wasn't thinking of Chick. I'm beginning to like Putty more and more. What she knows about the undercurrents in this town would be enough to write a saga."

"They live it up on Hagley Brow, do they?"

"And not only Hagley Brow, Shiner—She may not know what an alderman is. She may think the Borough Council was responsible for the nationalisation of the mines and the recession in the textile industry. But when it comes to personalities, she knows more than the Central Record Office. It looks as if I'm going to be fairly well tied up tomorrow, but I want you—amongst a dozen or so other things—to go out and see your elevated friend Sir Howard Who's-it, and try to get *his* version of the rise of Barson.

That is," Kenworthy said, "unless we're on our way back to London on the 10:14. You never can tell—and it wouldn't break my heart. Except for Putty, I'm not getting much joy out of Fellaby."

They entered the museum grounds, and Kenworthy stopped for a moment by the boarded window.

"Shiner—we must find out what the light was like on the famous night. Unless it was pitch dark, a man would have been a fool to have worked on that window from the outside. He'd be a prey to anyone chancing to pass the main gate."

They went round to the private door of the flat, and, not satisfied with prolonged pressure on the bell-push, Kenworthy hammered on the door with the side of his fist, so that the echoes reverberated from the walls of buildings in all parts of the town.

"If we're playing at Central European political police, there's no point in doing the job by halves."

There was no immediate reaction from above. For half a minute or so, Kenworthy allowed nocturnal peace to settle on the neighbourhood. Somewhere in the distance a dog began to bark and some creature scurried through the dry twigs of one of the bushes.

"Shiner—you'd better nip round the corner and make sure he doesn't do a bunk through the main door."

But at that moment a light appeared in one of the windows which Wright had been watching. There were footsteps coming and going along an upstairs passage. Kenworthy hammered again. The footsteps came down the stairs. There was a grinding of bolts and the sliding of a chain in its slot. The door opened, and Gill stood on the threshold, a shabby, plum-coloured dressing-gown over his faded blue pyjamas, his few straggling hairs ruffled over his bald head. He had not put on his glasses, and he peered at his visitors through eyes red and puffy with sleep. At the top of the stairs they saw a shapeless woman with her hair in rollers and a drab woollen cardigan thrown about the shoulders of her night-dress. Somewhere in the flat above they heard a child crying.

"We want to come in and talk," Kenworthy said. "It won't wait."

Gill preceded them up the stairs, his hands trembling, though it might have been with the cold. His wife stood aside to let them pass, her eyes frightened and questioning.

"Better go and look after the infant," Kenworthy told her. "We'll call you if we want you."

Gill took them into his study, a large, musty smelling room, untidy with books and curios. A chess end-game was laid out on a side-table, with a newspaper problem folded beside it.

"Gentlemen—I'm not surprised to see you here. I'm sure you know that.—But if you think I shot Barson, I was never out of the house that night. The Deputy Borough Treasurer and his wife were here. They brought some new records—"

There was an overwhelming smell in the room. He had made a mess in his pyjama trousers.

"I didn't come here to accuse you of shooting Barson," Kenworthy said, "or even to suggest that you had him shot. But there's a matter of withholding vital information, of obstructing the police in the performance of their duties, which has had the whole national net-work bogged down for the last twenty-four hours."

"I've been a fool," Gill said. "I never knew it would go as far as this. Even now, I can't convince myself that there's really any connection."

He was standing with his fingers jammed into his dressing-gown pockets. He had not remembered to ask the policemen to sit down. The room was like a refrigerator. Wright stooped down to plug in an electric bar fire.

"Look," Kenworthy said, "you'd better go and clean yourself up. Go with him, sergeant—no need to hang round his neck, but stay near enough—"

Kenworthy wandered casually round the study. The books were grimy, and thick dust lay along the upper edges of those in the higher open shelves. On the walls were unexciting reproductions of standard masterpieces and a few framed personal photographs; a younger and more eager Gill and his wife, leaning against a cairn with walking sticks in their hands; Gill, suitably intense, at the keyboard of a not very imposing church organ; Gill in the R.A.F., with a propeller on his arm and a smile for victory on his lips. That disposed of any connection with Barson's R.A.S.C. junketings.

Kenworthy picked up the printed report of a regional archaeological society and began to read it. Presently, Mrs. Gill came into the room, her hair roughly combed, carrying a tray with cups, milk and sugar.

"I hope you're not going to be too hard on William. If only you knew what we have suffered."

"It depends largely on what he has to tell us, and how frank he's prepared to be."

"He'll tell you everything. He's been dying to, ever since you've set foot in Fellaby."

"He's got an extremely curious way of setting about it."

"He's afraid he'll lose his job," she said.

"If he's afraid of no more than that, perhaps the prospects aren't so bad."

This startled her.

"What do you mean? Surely you don't think—"

"Ma'am, I'm two hundred odd miles away from home to investigate a murder. If what your husband has to tell me is a mere side-line, I doubt whether it'll interest me much."

Wright brought Gill back, and he had changed into a sportscoat and flannels, putting on a shirt with a collar, but no tie. He was wearing his spectacles now, and looked flustered still, but was a little more composed. He went over to the side-board and picked up a bottle of Johnnie Walker with not more than two doubles left in the bottom.

"Can I offer you gentlemen something a little stronger than coffee?"

"No, thank you."

"Do you mind if I have a drop?"

"If it'll help you to talk."

Mrs. Gill asked, "Do you want me here now?"

"Perhaps later."

She left them reluctantly, looking at her husband with a loving glance that Wright found pathetic.

Kenworthy spoke peremptorily.

"Come over here and sit down—on *this* chair—"

He wanted Gill near him. It was one of his principles, Wright knew, that some men found it harder to lie at close quarters. Gill sat forward, with his knees apart and his hands splayed over them.

"Now perhaps you will be kind enough to tell me what this is all about." .

"Do you mind if I begin at the beginning?"

"I'm not in the mood for spectacular originality."

"I was a young man when I first came to this town," Gill said, "young in mind, that is—young in heart, if you'll pardon a cliché."

It was difficult to imagine. But he had, at least, once climbed a Scottish mountain.

"That was before I met Barson.—I'm afraid you're not going to be impressed by what I shall tell you about our late leading citizen. I fear I shall not be able to make it very credible.—Barson was Chairman of the Library and Museum Committee when I was appointed—"

"Just a minute," Kenworthy asked, "have you any pronounced political views yourself?"

"Indeed, no. That would be most improper in my position. Of course, I have my personal opinions."

"Who hasn't?—Go on."

"Barson was chairman, and in the normal run of events would have presided over the sub-committee that appointed me. And here, at the risk of a digression, I must, if you are to understand Fellaby, give you some idea of the importance in the local mentality of these appointments sub-committees."

He was a little more settled now, talking fluently, speaking to a brief which he had run over in his mind many dozens of times. Kenworthy nodded patiently.

"They love it, superintendent. They love to sit there in their pomp and self-importance, conning over confidential references, asking personal questions, priding themselves that they've trapped the candidate on issues they know nothing whatever about. Believe me, superintendent, there's more bad blood, even amongst members of the same party, about who should sit on appointments sub-committees than there is about any other aspect of council business."

"I don't think Fellaby is unique in this respect."

"Perhaps not. But I think Barson was unique. He should

have been the chairman of my sub-committee, and I've no doubt he was looking forward to it with the usual relish. Moreover, I now know that he had his own pet candidate for the post—a young man from one of the Leeds libraries, a nice chap, though there was nothing outstanding in his qualifications. But Barson went down with influenza at the last moment. Kershaw had to take the chair, my present chairman, pleasant old fellow, Labour man, made his name in the Co-op. You can always rely on Kershaw to see fair play, and, though I say it myself, I was appointed. And I was very pleased. I liked Fellaby. I took over an efficient and loyal staff. There was this flat, which helped me over a tough housing problem."

And all the money he had saved up for mortgage deposit must have vanished into this uneconomical flat, with its vast floor space, its huge windows and its uncommonly difficult heating problem.

"Then Barson came back on the scene and found out what had happened. He made my life misery from then on. You've seen from the newspaper reports that he didn't like officials. He liked me less than any. The things you read refer only to formal, open meetings. You can have no idea what he was like in committee, when the press weren't present. Or even in the streets of the town.—He sneered, gentlemen. I forget of whom it was once written, he was born sneering. Barson was born sneering—at public librarians. Do you know that he once made a serious attempt to deprive me of this flat? He said the rooms ought to be taken in for additional display space. And he used to talk about 'the satisfied museum-going public of the pre-Gill era.' "

The hands of the clock stood at a quarter to three. Kenworthy interrupted gently.

"So. You disliked Barson. I dislike what I have learned about him. But someone disliked him enough to shoot him."

Gill made a gesture of despair.

"That this should have happened at this very time is a coincidence that appals me. It makes me feel to blame, and I keep telling myself that I am not to blame. You see, no man's tolerance is unlimited. There were times when I felt—I knew—that I could go on no longer. My wife will tell you. On the occasion when Barson moved a token reduction of my salary, we sat up halfway through the night, discussing the wisdom of my resigning without a job—or a home—to go to."

"So?"

"So—I had always suspected—a town like this has its whisperers, you know—it was often rumoured that not all Barson's dealings were above board. That's why I brought Warren in."

"Warren?"

"Your man in the green hat—a private detective—"

"You put Warren on to Barson?"

"My wife agreed to let me devote a substantial portion of our savings to this. I gave Warren £150 down, and the balance of £350 was payable the day Barson was convicted of corruption on evidence supplied by Warren.—Oh, I must ask you to believe me, gentlemen—I was not prepared to let him trump up a charge. It had to be fair, it had to be just. But I had little fear that we would fail. In point of fact—"

"Warren presented a verbal report to you that looked as if he were not so far off justifying your confidence?"

"That is right, superintendent. On the very day on which the Luger pistol was stolen from downstairs."

"You could have saved the country at large a hell of a lot of trouble if you'd come forward with this earlier," Kenworthy said.

"I know. I'm sorry, superintendent. I was afraid of finding myself under suspicion for the larger crime."

"There are several hundred other questions I shall want to ask you, and I'm afraid I shall have to ask them tonight. I shall anticipate, and take one of them out of turn, because it closely affects my programme of work for the next twenty-four hours.—Was there really any connection between Warren and Barson's military service?"

"No. That was only part of what he called his spiel."

"Good! It doesn't get us anywhere in particular, but at least it disposes of one issue.—All right, Mr. Gill, as I'm a family man myself, I'll let you go and fetch your good lady, and if it's any weight off your minds, you can tell her I believe every word you've said."

The little man stood up, and Wright saw that there was a

wet film across his eyes. In the interval whilst Gill was out of the room, Kenworthy began his ritual with his tobacco pouch.

"It had to be Warren, of all people. Do you remember the case, Shiner?"

"It doesn't ring a bell."

"Bloody buccaneer!" Kenworthy said, but before he could enlarge on the theme, Gill was back, bringing his wife, who was dabbing at her blotchy face with a totally inadequate lace-edged handkerchief.

"Superintendent Kenworthy, I'm so relieved—"

"We're not out of the wood yet," he said, "there still remains a mere case of murder—"

"Oh, please, superintendent—"

"—and I never could afford to believe in coincidence. I think we shall find a strong link between the murder of alderman Barson and the chain of enquiries which your husband set up, and which the mighty Mr. Warren pursued with characteristic verve. Which is why I'm anxious to stay here asking questions till dawn if necessary.—Now, first, how did you light upon the egregious Mr. Warren?"

"He advertises publicly. He works from Bradcaster, which is convenient. I'd heard some one in the library speak highly of him. And I thought—"

"That he wouldn't have any inhibitions about slipping his scalpel into high society?"

"I couldn't have put it as neatly as that."

"How long is it since you first contacted him?"

"About three months."

"Was he very eager to take the case?"

"Not at first. He hummed and ha'd about the distance from his base, and the dangers of queering his pitch with the wrong people."

"Even though what you were offering him was, when all's said and done, good money? After all, he could have had £150 for two days' work and an admission of failure. I suppose you paid the first instalment cash in advance?"

"A draft on the Post Office Savings Bank. But please don't get the impression that Warren did not give value for money. I was a little worried myself, because several weeks passed, and I had no word or sign of activity."

"You sent him a chaser?"

"I wrote him quite a firm letter, and he answered me by phone. Obviously he had had to clear a way through his current routine work. And then, he said, he had to do a fair amount of basic enquiry before he could actually start work on the ground."

"Did he contact you at all while he was operating in Fellaby?"

"Not until the afternoon you already know about."

"That was to present his final report?"

"No. He said his investigations had reached a certain point, but they weren't final. He had unearthed, he said, a number of potential charges, which he thought would stick. He promised me an interim report within the next few days—in writing."

"He asked you for more money?"

Gill did not answer at once. His wife was watching him tensely.

"Come along, Mr. Gill—I need to know."

"He didn't actually ask for more money. He did mention that his expenses were mounting up more than he had expected—"

"What sort of offences did he think he had discovered?"

"It all seems so very trivial, now. They were concerned with deliveries which the Highways Department was supposed to have made for use in Barson's garden."

"He had evidence enough on which to base these charges, had he?"

"He said he was nearly satisfied. There were just one or two other enquiries which remained to be made."

"I see. And when his statement of evidence was complete, who was going to launch the action? You, or Warren?"

"Oh, I would have taken that upon myself. It was part of our contract that Warren should fade out of the picture as soon as I was in a position to start proceedings."

"I'll bet it was. Warren would see to that."

Wright looked at the little man, slightly built, incongruously dressed, flushed with emotional manhandling. As Kenworthy had said, his story could be nothing but the truth. And this mild, harassed, bullied little curio-hunter

had been prepared to take on single-handed the moguls of
the borough.

"How would you have set about it?" Kenworthy asked.

"I would have seen the town clerk."

"Did Warren mention any other fiddles, other than the
one with the Highways Department?"

"There were one or two little things—sweetcners from
market stall-holders, gifts of bottles of spirits from licensees
when the Brewster Sessions were coming on, or when there
was an application for an extension of hours. But Warren
thought, and I agreed with him, that they would all have
been difficult to substantiate. It would have been difficult to
have felt sure of the witnesses, and in the outcome Barson
might have ridden the storm—distinctly to my disadvan-
tage.—I feel awful, talking about the man like this, now. I
had no idea that this would happen. I still don't see how
there can be any connection—"

"Did Warren give you the impression that he had stirred
up anything else—something a good deal more serious,
perhaps, but something he had no hope of proving?"

"Such as what, superintendent?"

"Well, something on a bigger scale than Fellaby. Some
bit of national roguery, for example? Something spreading
out into the county? Something to do with the places that
Barson visited in the course of his work?"

"No. There was no suggestion of anything like that."

"Did Warren say anything about Barson's two years in
the army?"

"No."

"Did you know anything at all about that period of his
life?"

"No, superintendent, really I didn't.—I still don't."

Kenworthy admonished him with the stem of his pipe.

"Mr. Gill, you've been very sensible up to now. And
until Barson was killed—which was none of your doing—
you showed nothing but pluck. You were prepared to take
on Barson—and his friends, if need be—single-handed.
You weren't scared. But you're scared now. You were too
easily satisfied—far too easily satisfied—when Barson
came to you with the story of the Highways Department.
When you set this affair in motion, you didn't think, did

you, that it was going to end up with a truck-load of paving-stones? When you squandered five hundred quid in the hope of hitting Barson for corruption, you must have known something. You must have suspected something a bit more serious that a few quids' worth of corporation stores. Now, I'm asking you, what was on your mind?"

Gill did not say anything. His wife looked disturbed.

"Let's approach it from another angle, Gill. Barson was, let's be honest about it, humble in his origins, blunt as to his intellect, mentally unbalanced. How does he go rocketing to the top in the choosiest party in the town?"

Gill licked his lips.

"That's an open secret. He was Sir Howard Lesueur's protégé."

"His nominee, you mean."

"If it makes any difference."

"But why, of all people, should Lesueur have picked on Barson?"

"How should I know? One man's as good as another, in that line of business, I should have thought—always provided he can be bought in the first instance."

"Exactly. And amongst other things, Lesueur runs the party in this district?"

"That is common knowledge."

"Because he can make or break them financially?"

"That's what people say."

"And as Lesueur's nominee, it was Barson's job to protect his master's interests as far as council business was concerned?"

"Indirectly, yes. And with due regard to constitutional practice. There has never been any suggestion of flagrant collusion."

"Nevertheless, when you commissioned Warren's investigation, it was in this sphere, wasn't it, that you really thought the story would break?"

"It had crossed my mind."

"You'd have had quite a single-handed fight on your hands, wouldn't you, laddie? A fight for which you've now lost your stomach."

"Now Barson's dead, I've no reason to go on fighting."

"All right, Mr. Gill—I'll go easy on you. Millions

wouldn't have had the guts· to start fighting, anyway. It would be rather like asking me to shop the Assistant Commissioner for smoking a cigarette that he's charged to entertaining guests. But I must persevere on one or two points. It's clear that when you were briefing Warren, you must have told him about the tie-up between Barson and Lesueur. If you hadn't mentioned it, it's clear that he'd have got round to it himself."

"I mentioned it."

"And how did Warren receive it? Gleefully?"

"He pulled a face about it. He said he hoped I wasn't going to get him baked in that sort of pie."

"And when Warren made his report to you the other day, did he mention the Lesueur angle?"

"Not at all."

"Did you ask him about it?"

"No."

"You were too happy to settle for a load of garden rubbish?"

"I suppose so."

Kenworthy eased his body in his chair.

"I think I would have been, too, laddie, if I'd been in your shoes.—Well, I shall want a full written statement from you, and I'm sure there's no need for me to bring you to the station to write it. You're a literate man. I take it you've got a typewriter? Just put down what you've told me, starting from that appointments subcommittee. You can omit any reference to Sir Howard Lesueur. There's no point in feeding that kind of poison into the local nick unless we have to."

He led Wright out into the frosty morning air. A heavy lorry was jolting through Fellaby. A couple of railway workers were walking with brisk, brittle steps towards the station.

"So the name Warren means nothing to you? I should have thought his name was printed on the lining of the heart of every detective sergeant."

"Who, or what, is he or was he?"

"A detective sergeant. With the Bradcaster City Borough Force. Hit the headlines about four years ago. Committed the cardinal sin for any detective sergeant—didn't report facts to his senior officers. Hung on to suspects in the hope that they'd lead him to solve big crimes off his own bat. There was also a strong suspicion that he could be bought off, and that he had a price for tip-offs. Nothing was ever proved. I was one of those that thought that Bradcaster didn't try very hard. Warren resigned without much fuss—he was sitting pretty, anyway—and Bradcaster counted their blessings."

"I think I remember the case. I must confess I'd forgotten his name."

"He was as crooked as a bent pin—and, to make him all the more dangerous—he was a damned fine detective. He set himself up in this private agency with a fair proportion of the Bradcaster records memorised, if not actually photo-copied. Also with four fifths of the Bradcaster informant service still in the palm of his hand, and probably several of his former mates, besides—always prepared to do them a service—on a strictly reciprocal basis. I always thought that Bradcaster were a little too happy to play the ostrich, once they were mercifully rid of Warren."

The Fellaby town hall clock struck five. They crossed the High Street. The County Hotel was already in view.

"So you can see how his eyes must have glistened, when Gill handed him the Barson case. Now I know that Warren was mixed up in it, it doesn't surprise me that things got worked up to murder pitch—though we've still to find the connection. You can bet your boots that Warren didn't tell Gill half of what he's dug up. Barson's garden path made a very convenient stopping place for stage one. But the rest Lesueur and the big stuff—Warren would have pigeon-holed for his own purposes. I wonder if Warren tried to put the screws on Barson himself?"

Kenworthy pressed the night bell at the County.

"I want to see you at the breakfast table at 7:45 sharp. That gives you roughly two hours—one in which to run over your notes of what Gill has told us. Don't bother to make a fair copy, but make sure it's all legible, that all your abbreviations and caballistic signs mean something. Nothing like going over your notes while they're still fresh in your memory. And try to get an hour's sleep, Shiner. Can't do a day's work without your proper rest."

• 8 •

OVER THE BREAKFAST table, Kenworthy briefed Wright in some quite surprisingly detailed aspects of the day's forthcoming interviews. He had even put ball-point to paper and listed some of the points which he wanted to make certain were not missed.

"Sorry to break my own rules and talk shop over bacon and eggs—but I've got to be away for most of the day. There are things I want you to keep jealously in our own hands. There are others that I want to saddle firmly and irretrievably on to the local boys."

"You'll be off to Bradcaster to see Warren?"

"Not half."

"You're not having him in?"

"What do *you* think? We haven't a shadow of a charge against him.—Feeling tired, boy?"

"Back of my neck's as stiff as a board, and there's half a yard of pump water where my spinal column ought to be. Otherwise I feel fit enough."

"Keep yourself going on cigarettes and coffee. Nine tenths of what you're going to do today will turn out to be irrelevant—that's always the way of it. But every thread has got to be unravelled, nevertheless."

Kenworthy conducted his morning conference with a briskness that had the shorthand writers on their mettle.

Gill was to be unobtrusively shadowed if he should leave the library premises—which was not considered likely. The press was to be played at arm's length over the green hat mystification: it was not yet sure that Warren would be easy to locate, so interest must be kept at least lukewarm. On the other hand, the name Warren was certainly not to be released. And Kenworthy did not release to his colleagues any suggestion of the Lesueur angle.

The collection, collation and analysis of questionnaires was to continue as if Gill had revealed nothing.

"Warren might," he said, "have let slip some detail on somebody's doorstep that could help us considerably."

He ordered a fresh neighbourhood enquiry about anyone who might have been seen in the vicinity of the museum on the night of the break-in. He asked for an inventory of all the known keys to the museum. Inspector Malpas had completed his initial investigation into *Futurco* and would present his report in a few minutes.

"Though I could have done with it last night," Kenworthy said.

"I didn't get back till late, sir. I thought you'd be in bed."

The town clerk had asked for an officer to call in the earlier part of the morning, and Wright would attend to that. The civic funeral was at 11:15, at which a strong contingent of the uniformed branch would be on parade and others, including sergeant Wright, would mingle with the crowd. Inspector Cook, formerly of the Military Police, would be over to expand his notes of the earlier Barson case; sergeant Wright would talk to him, at his convenience, during the course of the morning. Chief superintendent Grayling would himself co-ordinate arrangements for dealing with the pitched battle that was expected between the rival youth factions. For the rest, sergeant Wright had his orders, and would know how to fill in the odd corners of his day.

"There's a further point," Kenworthy said. "I notice that the broken window at the museum has not yet been glazed. Can someone ensure, please, that it remains as it is for the time being? I assume that the broken bits have been preserved?"

An officer of Grayling's staff nodded assent.

"I shall be asking for them—not necessarily today, though. I may not have time. Inspector Malpas, please—"

The officer who had accompanied Wright on his first visit to the museum put on his spectacles and went to the rostrum—one of the Sunday School's bible-boxes—and read what he had to say in flat, rapid tones.

"*Futurco Publicity* is a limited company, formed in 1934, and operating from second-floor offices in Eastgate Street, Bradcaster, which it has occupied since its inception. The senior personnel are Mr. Michael Endersley, Managing Director, Captain Lewis Exeter, Company Secretary, and the Rt. Hon. R. St. John Bradshaw, C.B.E., M.P., sleeping partner. The firm has exclusive rights of advertisement in the public service vehicles operated by the Bradcaster City transport undertaking and also owns hoardings in desirable sites both within the city and throughout the county.

"Edward Barson, subject of this enquiry, was employed by the firm since July 1954, at a salary rising by annual increments to the £1,850 per annum which he was earning just prior to his death. Invisible emoluments included private use of the firm's car, which was renewed annually, a mileage allowance, and fixed, tax-free expenses of £300 per annum.

"His work consisted of driving regularly about the area in which his company operated, examining the posters displayed on the company's hoardings, and reporting to his headquarters when any of these needed renewal, due to deterioration through age, weather or acts of vandalism. I understand that he carried out these duties to the complete satisfaction of his superiors."

Malpas closed his folder. Kenworthy looked at his watch, raised his hand in acknowledgement of the report, and tip-toed from the room.

Wright half rose in his chair.

"May I ask a question, please?"

"Certainly, sergeant."

"The common belief in Fellaby was that Barson acted as a middleman between commercial firms and the copy-writers who would actually produce their advertisements—"

"I could discover no substance in that. I can only assume that he invented such a story to give himself more imposing status among his acquaintances in this town."

"Do you happen to know, sir, what work he did before he went to *Futurco*?"

At least half a dozen policemen showed eagerness to reply.

"Before he was called into the armed forces, he was a

trainee fitter at Morley's—that's a light engineering firm along the Town Moor Road. After demobilisation, he acquired a small insurance book, and went about the outlying villages on a bicycle."

Malpas sat down. Grayling picked up his gloves and swagger cane and went back to his office. Rhys took charge of the Report Centre, assigning officers to details, and issuing commands that Wright considered unnecessarily noisy in his chanting, Welsh voice. Wright went up to him and formally asked to be dismissed.

"You have your orders for the day from superintendent Kenworthy? And you don't require assistance from any of my officers?"

Wright made his way to the town hall and found the town clerk staring motionless and moody out of his window, as if he had maintained the same stance since the detectives had last been there. But he was now dressed entirely in coarse and uncompromising black, and his wig stood ready on a wooden stand by his desk.

"So. An hour before the funeral it has to be. I fear that there has been no error in the Borough Engineer's paperwork. I have personally interviewed the yard foreman and several other of our municipal employees, and certain admissions have been made. There have been thefts—not on an alarming scale, but thefts, nevertheless, and a somewhat ingenious juggling of the books to conceal the discrepancies. It goes without saying that I shall prosecute. If you wish to begin taking statements—"

"No, sir. Superintendent Kenworthy and I have our hands full with the main concern. We shall have to leave this issue to be attended to by the local station. Unless—"

"Unless what, sergeant?"

"Unless you think, Mr. Belfield, that there are likely to be ramifications. That is, unless any further and more extensive improper practices come to light."

"And what do you think they are likely to be, sergeant?"

"We don't know, sir. We merely feel that where this kind of thing has been going on on a small scale—and where events have already reached the pitch of fatal violence—there may well have been other malpractices."

"I can hardly think what they would be. Anything bigger

than the case in hand would certainly have been revealed at our annual audit, or in one of our frequent snap-checks. But believe me, sergeant, the moment this funeral is over, this town hall is going to be turned inside out. If anything else untoward has been going on, I can assure you that you shall hear about it."

He came back to his desk and sat down with his hands laid wearily on his blotter.

"There's a bitter irony about it, sergeant. One of our promising young quantity surveyors might very likely go to prison over this. He will certainly lose his job, and it is equally certain that he is a ruined man as far as a career in local government is concerned. Two other employees, with thirty-five years of trouble-free service between them, are going to get the sack. And I can't help feeling for them. I know what they were up against. With Barson at their throats, they hardly stood a chance. And what did Barson stand to gain out of all this? By the time he'd sweetened everybody who needed to be sweetened, it must have cost him as much as if he'd bought his paving-stones on the open market. It's as if he had to do it the underhand way for the sheer challenge of it."

"Superintendent Kenworthy and I had arrived at precisely that reading of his character, sir."

"Well—you haven't been in Fellaby long—but you don't seem to have missed much. And do I gather that I am shortly also likely to have to advertise for a new librarian?"

"From our point of view, I don't think that will be necessary, sir. We are of course not concerned with his obvious transgressions of protocol, which are purely your domestic affair. The superintendent did ask me to suggest to you that Gill might well be encouraged to take a few days' leave."

"That will be convenient for all parties.—Have your investigations given you a realistic picture, I wonder, of what Gill has had to tolerate?"

"They have indeed."

"I rather like the little man," the town clerk said. "Perhaps he will be able to settle down to enjoy life, when this has blown over.—Will that be all, sergeant?"

"Kenworthy did ask me if you could give us a line—

entirely off the record, of course—on Sir Howard Lesueur."

The town clerk blew out his cheeks and exhaled air through protruded lips.

"Lesueur? I don't know the man. Oh, I've met him—I'm always meeting him—at receptions and the like. But he's not an easy man to know, and I've never felt constrained to try particularly hard. I've never really tried, in twenty-five years. I drink his whisky. I eat his wife's canapés, I've even had my back slapped by him. But Lesueur is a politician, and I'm not. I do my best to keep this town on an even keel despite the politicians. Up to now, I pride myself that I've succeeded, by and large."

"What do you think will happen, sir, if there's a change of political control on your council?"

"Oh—has someone been talking to you about the intrigues to put councillor Durkin into an alderman's seat?—A lot will happen, sergeant, and in the long run not very much.—And I hope you can soon release me, now. I'm due to go down to the Mayor's Parlour in five minutes' time, ready for our procession."

"The superintendent wanted me to ask your opinion on one other small matter, sir—but it can wait. I can come back later."

"What is it?"

"We've formed an impression of alderman Barson with which you don't seem to disagree. We can't help wondering what such a man must have been like as a husband and father."

The first note of the parish church's passing bell struck dismally across the street outside.

"For that, sergeant, you'll have to go to the gossips—of whom you'll find no short supply. It isn't that I won't tell you—I simply can't. I don't pry, and I don't listen to old women. If you think the opinions of the Carlton estate are worth having, you might try over there."

He stood up. And then he made a remark which was to haunt Wright until Kenworthy told him the answer.

"There is something, and you'll come across it sooner or later. And when you do, you'll not blame me for not having mentioned it to you."

•9•

WRIGHT LEFT THE town hall as major elements in the procession were being manoeuvred into position in a side-road; the Boys' Brigade, with black crêpe arm-bands and their drums muffled; a contingent of nursing cadets; a representative Civil Defence team; a platoon from the British Legion, wearing medals dating from before Barson's birth. Wright came abreast of the doorway in which the crippled newspaper-seller sat hunched, his trousers thread-bare and shapeless against his withered leg. There were no papers in his stand at this time of day, but he had a tray of match-boxes and shoe-laces, to which no one was paying attention.

Wright moved into the doorway with him. There was plenty of room; it was not a popular position. The newsman would not be able to see anything of the procession, only the backs of the people in front of him.

"A fair send-off for the most unchristian man in Fellaby," the cripple said. "It shocks you, doesn't it, to hear me talk like that? Well, I can afford to speak my mind. I've had more than my share of suffering."

"What did he ever do to you?" Wright asked.

"Breathe out in the same air that I have to breathe in."

The single doleful bell was still reverberating at long intervals across the roofs of the town. They heard a shout of command from the subaltern of a platoon of Territorials.

"You'll have to tell me about him, sometime. I'm sorry I can't stay now. I'm supposed to be at the cemetery."

The deformed man caught Wright's cuff as he stepped out of the doorway.

"I know what I'm talking about, sergeant. I could tell you a thing or two. I was at school with him."

Wright moved sideways like a crab, rubbing shoulders with the shop-fronts and the crowd. Beyond the shopping street, outside the terrace houses, the bystanders were thinner. Chairs and benches had been set against the edges of the gutter.

In the little road that led up to the cemetery, police were on duty, diverting people who wanted to park their cars. Windows were wound up in bursts of bad temper, and drivers took it in turn, with ill grace, to reverse into an entry. As Wright approached, Lesueur arrived in a gleaming Mercedes-Benz, and was signalled to a place by the kerb. The chauffeur pulled the nose of the vehicle across the narrow road to back down ready for departure.

Someone touched Wright's sleeve.

"Sergeant Wright?"

"Speaking."

"My name's Cook. Inspector. Other side of the Pennines, I've got the dope on that Bad Siebenhausen affair."

"After this, sir, if you wouldn't mind. We'll find somewhere for a coffee. If you'll bear with me while I make a couple of phone calls first?"

"Of course. I gather you're up to your ears in it?"

"Battling."

The inspector was a tall man, broadly built, with a fresh, red, boyish face. He waved a hand to take in a whole décor of the funeral.

"Bad business, eh?"

"Mixed bag. You knew him in his earlier days."

"Not changed, I expect?"

"Not for the better, as far as we can make out."

The civic cortège began to arrive, the bands, cadets and hangers-on left outside the gate. The mayor's chain was tied to his shoulders with bows of black ribbon. One of the undertaker's men rearranged the folds of the Union Jack over the coffin.

"Ex-serviceman," Wright said.

"When I took a statement from him, he was just one week out of a pox hospital."

The family mourners supported each other into the

church, behind them the more distant relatives, well
equipped in funeral finery, little grief in their faces.

"How do you like working with Kenworthy?"

"It's the first time I've been out of London with him.
He's a fair bloody handful."

"I notice he's been able to swing himself clear of this
noble bit of pageantry."

"He's out of town. Gone to check up on Warren."

"Warren? Not Warren of Bradcaster?"

"I suppose there is only one Warren in Bradcaster. The
one who used to be in their C.I.D."

"What's Warren got to do with this case?"

"Someone called him in as a private eye to try to shop
Barson."

O God, our help in ages past came swelling from the
church, the congregation a bar and a half behind the
organist.

"Bloody hell!" Cook said.

"I hadn't heard of Warren before. Kenworthy seems to
think he's dangerous."

"Dangerous!—Listen! He had the luck of the nine blind
bastards. It staggered me that they let him resign. But if
they hadn't, he'd have pushed the pillars of the temple
down. There'd have been some epoch-making changes in
Bradcaster."

"And he cuts some ice as a free-lance?"

"It stands to sense, doesn't it? Provided that he plays it
reasonably cool, he can do what he wants with either side.
And if he'd rumbled Barson, no wonder someone had to
remove the evidence.—Bloody chilly, isn't it?"

They walked together between the rows of wreaths that
lined the path from the church to the grave-side. Some of
the spectators had begun to drift away, now that the most
impressive pomp was over. Wright and Cook moved nearer
to the church porch.

"It's not generally known, is it, that Kenworthy is on to
Warren?"

"No. Not outside the Report Centre."

"You'll have to keep your eyes peeled, once the news
breaks. Somebody in this town is going to be up to the ears

in it.—And you must be out on your feet. Someone told me that you were up all night."

"I'll get by."

Wright knew that fatigue would come over him in waves at intervals during the day. At the moment, the cold and his mental alertness had him on an upward curve.

Cook nodded towards the church.

"It'll be a bloody sight warmer in there," he said.

They walked quietly into the porch, and a sidesman, mistaking them perhaps for weightier personages than they were, opened the felt-covered door with the merest creak of its hinges and beckoned them inside with his forefinger on his lips.

The bishop had been brought in to take the service, and in his purple cassock, with frills of lace at his wrist, was preaching about the self-sacrifice of those who dedicated their lives to public service. There were seasonal coughs among the congregation. Many were standing at the back of the church. The brass plate on Barson's coffin was catching a ray of pre-spring sunshine that slanted across the southern transept.

"If it had been given to our brother to complete the work which he had with such exultant promise begun—"

A number of unecclesiastical ways of finishing the sentence crossed Wright's mind, and he guessed that Cook would also be making the most of its possibilities. As silently as he could, he reached for the handle of the door and let himself out into the frostiness. Cook followed him, the thick herringbone material of his greatcoat rubbing against the door-post.

"Going to stay for the graveyard stuff?"

"I'd better, just in case there's an accident."

"Whose is the big car?"

"The squire. The man who pulled Barson's strings."

"Name?"

"Lesueur."

"Don't know him. Still, there's one in every community."

They watched the committal ceremony from a discreet distance and then left the cemetery in time to be ahead of the main body. Wright thought better of his plan to entertain

Cook in one of Fellaby's more respectable cafés, deciding that they were likely to be over-worked on account of the crowds in town.

"I think we'd better go back to the nick," he said. "And I'm afraid I'll have to do my telephoning before we get down to business. I'm sorry to keep you hanging about like this. I'm sweating blood trying to fit everything in."

"Not to worry, son. This is a day out for me. We can talk as we walk along."

"I think it would be better to wait until I can sit down and take full notes. Kenworthy's a stickler."

His first call was to New Scotland Yard. He wanted to know from inspector Heather whether check had yet been made of the recent movements of Barson's army associates. Heather treated him to a verbal display that almost seared the wires.

"Will you ask superintendent Kenworthy if he thinks this department is something out of *Softly, Softly?*—"

But the job had been done. The men had been cleared.

Next, Wright went to see Grayling, who had by now returned by car from the cemetery. The austere commander of the division had his desk strewn with dusty rosters.

"I don't know how we're going to do it, sergeant. There isn't a man on the station who'll get a rest day this week. Treble town patrol this morning; a parade; a Report Centre to man; all these questionnaires; eight officers in court; now a pitched battle to be catered for in the High Street."

"I'm afraid I've not come to bring you any relief, sir."

Wright outlined the nature of the charges that the town clerk would be laying.

"Blast it, sergeant—I don't know whom I can spare. And yet I mustn't keep the Borough waiting. This means as inspector and a sergeant. And it isn't really germane to your main issue, is it?"

"We think not, sir."

"Well, I've no choice. I'll ask Malpas to go over. All right, sergeant, thank you."

Wright then used the C.I.D. phone to call Fellaby Moor Hall. It took some patience with a servant to bring Sir Howard to the phone in person. But the man was extremely civil, remembered their brief meeting in the County, sounded even interested. Would Wright come over to the Hall for tea?

As he replaced the receiver, Wright realised that there were beads of sweat on his forehead. Cook looked at him across the little office.

"Don't let it kill you, sergeant. After all, you're only working on one case. Back home I'm in the middle of a dozen. Are you ready for my little story now?"

Wright turned to a fresh page in his note-book.

"I don't know how much of this is likely to interest you, but it'll help you to get to know Barson. His unit was one which we'd had our eyes on for a long time. A long time before Barson was called up—right back, in fact, to a few weeks after D-Day, when they opened up a supply dump at a roadhead in Belgium. One of their main activities—and one of their main sources of fiddling—was to receive large consignments of motor-cycles from England and distribute them to units in the field. It didn't take us long to discover that quite a frightening number of these machines were finding their way to the civilian market. It was quite remarkable what you could do with an army bike, once you got rid of its khaki paint and put a bit of chrome on its silencer and gear-box cover. They fetched a hell of a price, too—well, you can imagine."

Cook offered Wright a cigarette, took one himself, and flicked the match in the general direction of an open fire-place stuffed with old newspapers.

"We ran a few of these machines down, but we were never able to prove anything. The presiding genius was a lieutenant, whose name you've already got—the one who's been playing parliament. It was only a tiny little section that was involved, in an otherwise impeccable unit, and they must have cleared up a bloody packet. It worked well enough while the war lasted, and even for some months afterwards. But demobilisation broke the original team up. New faces appeared, new men, that the lieutenant did not know whether he could trust or not. One of these was Barson. Barson looked a likely lad, was made up to corporal, was cut in on the deal. There weren't as many machines to dispose of, now, but such as there were found as ready a market in occupied Germany as anywhere else."

Cook tapped cigarette-ash into an empty tobacco tin on the wooden table.

"The trouble was, Barson had ideas of his own, Barson was a big-head, a clever bugger. He had to show the old-timers he could go one better than they could. I shall never forget the first time I questioned him. He treated me with complete contempt, that's the only phrase I can find for it. And even when he found himself under close arrest, he was still as blasé as ever—still had that bloody sneer on his lips, seemed to know from the start he was going to get away with it. And, of course, he did—because I put my bloody great foot in it, out of over-anxiety to shop the bugger."

"We heard about that—a technicality—"

"I ought to have known better. Things might have come out differently, even in Fellaby, if I had. Barson wasn't content with flogging bikes that the section had fiddled through their books. He started pinching other people's. Despatch riders were under strict standing orders to remove the leads from their sparking-plugs, whenever they left their machines unattended. But spare leads were no difficulty to Barson. He had half a dozen in his kit when we searched it. He must have had some wild night rides—he took some skin-of-his-teeth chances—and enjoyed every minute of it. He stole bikes of makes that R.A.S.C. didn't handle. In at least two cases their riders were court-martialled for negligence in losing them. And Barson started under-selling his own confederates—to the same dealer who had carried out most of their transactions."

"Who was probably no stranger to you people—"

"The German civil police had had him under surveillance for some time, but he was pretty fly. He was one of those cases you know well enough from your own experience—everyone knows, everyone's been dying for years to clap iron on him, but there's never a second witness to put in the box."

"I'd better have this German's name," Wright said, "in case he harboured a grudge."

Inspector Cook read from his notes.

"Kurt Fischer, *Auto-betrieb Fischer,* Bad Siebenhausen, Walsroder Landstrasse 7, Rhine-Westphalia.—To come back to Barson: he went a step too far. He nicked one of my section's bikes—from outside a guard-room in a military compound. And he'd started getting careless over details: little things, like filing serial numbers off engine-parts. We found the bike at Fischer's and were able to identify it. Fischer talked, volubly. We got a list of payments that he'd made for machines received."

"Surely they found it difficult to dispose of all this foreign currency?"

"They didn't take payment in money, you understand. They stuck to convertible property: watches, jewellery, cameras, binoculars, ciné projectors. Fischer was systematic. He gave us an inventory, chapter and verse. And we found a lot of it in their kit. And *I*, bloody fool, was so almighty eager that I searched their quarters in their absence. The whole case fell down."

"Couldn't you have charged them nevertheless? You'd got Fischer's statement. You'd got the loot."

"I don't know how intimate you are with British court martial procedure, sergeant. Of all systems of justice in the world, it's the one most heavily weighted in favour of the prisoner. Fischer's word against theirs was uncorroborated, and he was a shady character, to put it mildly. The Judge Advocate-General's department gave my C.O. a rocket that made military history, and this was duly passed on to us, adequately condensed, concentrated and rarefied."

"So Fischer got away with it, too?"

"We dropped the lot. Eight of us were handling sixteen murders, two dozen rapes and eleven abortions simultaneously.—And that's about all I can tell you. I don't see it's going to be much use to you. But they asked me to come over, and it's made a change."

Wright ate shepherd's pie in the police canteen, and the black coffee which followed it brought some new lease of wakefulness to his arteries. Then he put through another call to inspector Heather.

"No, sergeant—I have not yet finished my longhand copy of the nominal roll of Barson's army company."

"It isn't that, sir. This is one for Interpol. Kurt Fischer, sometime garage proprietor, Bad Siebenhausen, Rhine-

Westphalia. Could you get them to advise present where-abouts and recent journeys, please?"

"Making progress, are we, sergeant?"

"No, sir."

Wright hung up with the curtest of acknowledgements. Then he found a shorthand typist in the Report Centre who was sufficiently off her guard to let him dictate a summary of what Cook had told him. He did not think it was likely to serve any great purpose, but it was the sort of thing that Kenworthy was likely to ask for for no particular reason and without notice. In the event, Kenworthy was often to claim, when he talked about the case afterwards, that it was this statement which enabled them to make their ultimate break-through.

· 10 ·

THREE OF THE vehicles which Wright attempted to requisition to take him out to Fellaby Moor Hall were diverted before he could take advantage of them. Onc was sent out six miles to a by-pass to cut off a hit-and-run driver. The second was put at the disposal of inspector Malpas, to take him to the corporation stock yard, three hundred yards away. The crew of the third were told off to attend the chief superintendent's briefing conference on the show-down of the Stanway gang.

"Why do you want a car to take you up to Fellaby Moor?" the desk sergeant asked him. "There's a bus service every hour and a half. Next one at five past three."

The positive result, as far as Wright was concerned, was that he missed the hour on his bed which he had promised himself after lunch. His eye-lids were heavy as he sat on a wooden bench on the bus station, and the backs of his hands and fingers tingled with fatigue.

The bus was a single-decker with upholstery worn thin and packed tight. In the low gears, which it had to maintain to climb the steep hills out of town, every window rattled in its frame and every bolt and rivet of its coach-work seemed loose in its housing. Over the crest of Coal-Pit Lane Wright looked down at half a square mile of similar streets, laid out with geometrical precision, differentiated only by the endless variety of the smoking chimney-pots, or by the bound-breaking exuberance of some householder who had painted his front door lemon yellow or Cambridge blue.

Then they were free of Fellaby. The road still climbed, between hedge-bottoms sodden with February rain, past

clustered farm-steads that wrested a living from poor soil
and steeply contoured fields.

Fellaby Moor Hall was at the end of a long drive, over
cattle-grids, across a quarter mile of sweeping park land.
The house was a battlemented Elizabethan manor, built in
the form of a hollow square whose wings overlooked the
broad sweep of steps leading up to its main door. It was a
grim building, as dour as the land-scape which fathered it,
with tall, stately, leaded windows, and edged with rose-
beds that must, in season, have been a show-piece. In a
tightly restrained manner, it was not inelegant.

A woman-servant in her middle sixties showed Wright
into an immense stone-flagged hall that could have been a
blue-print for a newer and better Fellaby museum, so
replete was it with oak settles, oil paintings, heraldry and
ancient sporting prints. On the wall was a tombstone brass
of a Crusader in armour which Wright was sure must have
been pillaged from some parish church.

Sir Howard was standing with his agent beside an
enormous open fire in which flames were licking the bark
off half a tree. He was wearing tailor-cut trousers of cavalry
twill, a sports-coat with leather guards at cuffs and elbows,
a yellow waistcoat with an overlaid pattern of red check and
a spotted bow tie. Colonel Hawley was in riding breeches
and a hacking jacket, his calves encased in knee-length
leather leggings.

"Ah! Come in, Wright! I don't know whether you've met
the colonel? Damned fine show I think they put on this
morning. Not bad at all for Fellaby. I thought the bishop
laid it on in the right places, too."

He turned to dismiss Hawley.

"I'll leave that to you, then. Get in touch with Jevons. If
Burroughs is going to be awkward, play for time. Get it
shelved until the next monthly meeting.—Now, sergeant,
my good lady is waiting for us upstairs."

He conducted Wright along a corridor flanked with
statuary and armoured breast-plates.

"I keep meaning to get rid of half this junk. Must give it
to Gill. Damn it, I gave them the building. I ought to give
them something worth putting in it."

They went up a narrow, wooden, spiral staircase, so dark

and unguarded that Wright felt forward with his toes on every tread. Lesueur lifted the latch of a studded door and showed him into a room in which his wife was waiting with towering piles of buttered scones and home-made cake.

It was a large, square room in the west wing, overlooking the main forecourt, and here ancient and modern met in a superb unity of rarity and comfort. Small, oval eighteenth century miniatures decorated the walls. There was a Sheraton writing-desk that must have been beyond price and an inlaid coffee-table on which Wright was afraid to set down his plate. At the same time, he counted four night-storage heaters ranged round the walls, and the shuttered cabinet of the television set must have been custom-made at a price that run into hundreds.

Lady Lesueur was younger than her husband, a small but well filled-out figure in a brown skirt, with black hair tinged with wisps of grey. She was wearing fur-lined ankle boots, as if even the cosiest of tea-parties was an interruption in the outdoor round.

"You know, Mr. Wright, I was saying to Sir Howard, I think I must have been everywhere there is to go, and yet this is the first time I've actually met a man from Scotland Yard."

"You move in the wrong circles, my dear."

"I find it wonderfully exciting," she said. "Do you take milk, Mr. Wright? I'll leave you to put the sugar in yourself."

"Damned shame that the excitement had to take this kind of turn. Pity they didn't get Durkin instead!"

"Oh, Howard! What a thing to say! You must forgive my husband, Mr. Wright! He practises fire-eating in front of the bathroom mirror every morning. But it doesn't really come naturally to him—Sandwiches? Egg and cress, smoked salmon, pâté—"

"The trouble is," Lesueur said, "I'm still not myself about this. I was fond of Edward Barson. Doesn't seem the right thing to say, but I did make him what he was, you know. I'd nurtured that boy. Right from his coming out of the army, I'd taken him under my wing. You could see it in him, you know—energy, integrity, loyalty. And what a way he had to go still, what a mark he'd have made. He wouldn't have stopped at Fellaby, you know. Just another three years, I told him, only last week, and they'd have been pleading with him to go to Westminster."

The sandwiches were tiny, crustless, triangular. Wright seemed to have eaten three of them whilst his hosts were still nibbling at their first.

"Character!" Lesueur said. "That's what he had. It doesn't come all too often, these days. And he had to be cut down by some little yobbo who ought to have been birched on the day of his birth. I don't know why you people haven't slapped the manacles on him and signed the whole thing off. But then, you've got this red herring of a pip-squeak in the sloppy hat, haven't you?"

Wright tried to imitate Kenworthy's gentler tones.

"There's no conclusive evidence against Stanway," he said, "and we can't discount the activities of this other figure."

"Toasted tea-cake, Mr. Wright—or scone?"

"Give him both!" Lesueur thundered. "Can't you see the man has an appetite?"

Wright was sorry to be diverted from the pâté sandwiches, which he found supremely palatable. He opted for the tea-cake.

"This is one of the things I'm afraid I have to ask you, sir. Did he come here?"

"Did who come here?"

"This mysterious character in the felt hat?"

"What in thunder would he want to come here for?"

"Perhaps I ought not to tell you this, sir—but the papers will have it before long. We have reason to believe that this visitor was a private detective hired to gain information about alderman Barson."

"Some socialist stunt, I don't doubt. Looking for a smear-story. And if they couldn't find one, they'd invent one. Well—he didn't come here. If he had, I'd have booted his arse from here to the duck-pond!"

"Howard!"

"You didn't see anything of this crawler, did you?"

"No. Certainly he didn't call when I was in. I can ask the servants. Have some jam, Mr. Wright?"

"What sort of thing would he want to be pinning on to Barson, anyway?"

"Oh, I don't know, sir. The alderman's views didn't appeal to all shades of opinion."

"You're not one of these damned reds, are you, sergeant?"

"No, sir. I try not to be anything. But as an impartial observer, there are one or two aspects of alderman Barson's career that interest me."

"Such as?"

"Well, sir—I don't know how best to express this—one wouldn't perhaps have looked on him as conventional material for preferment in your party, would one?"

"Wouldn't one?"

Lesueur's slight stress on the pronoun was scornful.

"Wouldn't one? Because he struggled up out of the slums, you mean? Young man—your brain is constipated with theory, and you've sat on the fence so long that you're in danger of bisecting yourself. You talk ideas, but I don't think you've any idea of facts. Somebody's told you that Barson came from the slums. But does that really mean anything to you? Do you really know what those slums were like? Do you know that they'd only one outside tap for eight houses in Kenilworth Street? That they'd an outside lavatory that was frozen solid for two months of every year? Have you ever lived in a Fellaby slum, Wright?"

"Two kinds of cake," Lady Lesueur said.

Wright chose a light looking sponge, his fingers sinking into thick cream as he tried to lift a slice from the plate.

"Do you know that Barson won a scholarship to the local grammar school, but his father wouldn't let him take it? In case he should give himself airs? Do you wonder that he grew up with some strong opinions? That he couldn't tolerate those who'd had a better chance than he had, but hadn't taken advantage of it?—Oh, I know Edward Barson was impulsive. He spoke sometimes and thought afterwards. There were times when he had us all sitting on the edge of our seats, wondering what was coming next. But do you think we wanted that brain, that oratory, that fearlessness, to go over to the other side? Do you know that Kenilworth Street now returns a conservative councillor?

And can you guess whom we have to thank for that? Don't you think there's room in my party for a few red-blooded progressives who still haven't turned their backs on the establishment? Don't you know that that's where the floating vote is floating to now, because there aren't a few Barsons on the Treasury benches?"

"I shall be personally offended, Mr. Wright, if you don't try this other cake as well. I baked it myself. This is none of your packet mixtures."

"But when you made him an alderman—" Wright began, as persuasively as he could.

"*I* didn't make him an alderman. *I'm* not a Fellaby Borough councillor. I was made mayor by invitation in coronation year—but that's a constitutional prerogative of the corporation. I'm chairman of the divisional association. I see fair play whilst others fight out the policy decisions. But I play no active part in politics. It was the Fellaby borough councillors who made Barson an alderman."

"And when they did, sir—did they not pass over several others who, by virtue of seniority—"

"The decision was unanimous. By the whole party caucus. May I also add, it was spontaneous? I cannot remember that they even consulted me. And is there so much harm in demonstrating that ours can be a young man's party?"

"Another cup of tea, Mr. Wright?"

Lesueur brought a silver cigarette-box from an occasional table.

"Have a cancer-stick!"

"I'm afraid that one bit of unpleasantness has gone so far that we can't stop it, sir."

"Oh?"

Wright was speaking closely to the brief which Kenworthy had given him at the breakfast table. He gave an unembroidered account of the affair of Barson's garden-path, omitting any reference to Gill or Warren. Lesueur was very angry.

"You people just can't help stirring things up, can you?"

"Poor Mrs. Barson!" Lady Lesueur said. "Naturally, you aren't letting it go any further."

"It's out of our hands."

"That's what you always say. I'll have a word with Grayling about it."

"It's beyond superintendent Grayling's control, sir. The papers will have to go to the Director of Public Prosecutions. The town clerk—"

"Blast the town clerk! What are you aiming to do—put a corpse in the dock?"

"It isn't a question of that, sir. There's a charge of falsifying public accounts."

"By whom?"

"By an employee of the borough—a quantity surveyor—"

"Well—there are ways and means of covering that, surely? Somebody's made a mistake, a clerical error. How much was involved? Fifty quid at the most? Sack the man, kick him upstairs, get him a better job. Soon fix *him*."

Wright smiled. He wondered whether Kenworthy would have permitted himself a moment's quiet provocation.

"Sounds remarkably like compounding a felony," he said softly.

"You can call it what you like, sergeant. You fellows have a high-sounding phrase for everything. Well, you go ahead, do your worst! I shall personally see to it that your efforts are stopped at source. And in doing so, I shall not be perverting the course of justice—I shall be cultivating it. I am not going to stand by and see that young man's name besmirched."

Lady Lesueur began to gather up empty plates and cups, as if the tap of her hospitality had been turned off.

"If I could broach just one more topic, sir."

Wright was beginning inwardly to curse Kenworthy's brief. He did not believe that even the superintendent would continue to press his luck in the face of Lesueur's last outburst. There were, it was obvious, several reasons why Lesueur ought not to be antagonised at as early a stage as this. Nevertheless, Wright pursued his course.

"Been wallowing in some other cess-pool, have you, sergeant?"

"No, sir. And I apologise for putting these questions to you. But we are here to investigate a murder—"

"One would hardly think it. It would seem that the main object of the exercise is to denigrate a murdered man."

"Not at all, sir. The man who killed him must have been his enemy. We have to find out who his enemies were, and to do that we have to find out as much as we can about his character and habits."

"If you follow that to its natural conclusion, you'll go out immediately and arrest the leader of the opposition on Fellaby Council."

"Not necessarily, sir. There are more facets to a man's personality than his politics. His work, for example."

"I don't think you'll find anything exceptional in Barson's work."

"And his domestic circumstances?"

"What have they to do with it?"

"I'm not saying they have anything to do with it. It's just—well—I think we're all agreed that Barson was not an easy character. You said yourself, just now, he was impulsive. I've met his wife—his widow—and she seemed a pleasant, courageous uncomplicated soul—"

"Sergeant—this is too much! By God, this is too much!"

"Outrageous!" Lady Lesueur said.

"We have to consider every possibility. Even a negative response might be informative."

"I refuse to discuss the matter a moment longer. I shall speak to the Chief Constable and make sure that I am not importuned again except by a responsible officer. And I don't care if the Chief Commissioner of the Metropolitan Police were to come up here himself: I would refuse to try to wring evidence out of a dead man's home life. I think this is perfectly monstrous!"

"I'm sorry, sir, I—"

"Sorry be damned! You're sorry you're going to get no empty gossip out of me, that's all you're sorry about. And now you must excuse me, sergeant. I have work to do."

Wright negotiated the spiral stairs with stumbling feet, the treads too narrow for the soles of his shoes; his heels catching in the uneven crevices.

He walked disconsolately along the long drive back to the village, whose dour stone houses huddled together under skeletal trees. Half way along he stepped sideways to make way for a battered red shooting-brake. Colonel Hawley's lips smiled up from under his brisk, military moustache.

"You're looking down in the mouth, sergeant. Did he give you a rough time?"

Wright screwed up his face, and could not think of a safe immediate answer.

"If you've just broken the news to him that was whispered to me in the town hall ten minutes ago, I'm not surprised. Bloody bad show all round, isn't it?"

"I must say, I'm not enjoying this case."

"You're not going to enjoy walking back to Fellaby, either, are you?"

"I'll wait for the bus."

"No more today. Tuesdays and Saturdays only. You ought to read the small print at the foot of the time-table, sergeant."

Hawley swept aside a pile of countryman's paraphernalia—a bundle of drain-cleaning rods and field glasses in a leather case—from the passenger seat, and reversed, with his back wheels over the rough grass.

"Hop in!"

They swept over the stone bridge that crossed the village's shallow torrent. Hawley lit a cheroot.

"So his Nibs is all for letting sleeping garden-paths lie, is he?"

Wright decided that it was worth the risk of tackling the main line.

"He thinks all that is unnecessary muck-raking," he said, "but that's not what upset him."

"Oh?"

"I tried to get a line on Barson's private life. He didn't like it."

"He wouldn't.—But you could get a line on Barson's private life without skewering Lesueur's lapel. Plenty of people in Fellaby—"

"Not up to now. When I bring it up, people go all coy."

"You must have been meeting the wrong people."

They came into Fellaby, passing a wide street-corner that had been cleared for development and then apparently forgotten, for dried regiments of last year's rose-bay willow-herb guarded the rubble, and against the outside walls of houses that had escaped the bulldozers, weathered laminations of wall-paper spread in dampened patches beside fire-places open to the winds.

"Perhaps you'd be one of the right people," Wright ventured.

Hawley laughed, curtly and without humour.

"Oh, leave me out of it, sergeant, if you don't mind.— Oh, I'd help you, if I thought it would do you a ha'porth of good. And if you haven't got what you want in twenty-four hours, come and see me again. But don't involve me if you can help it. After all, I *am* the conservative agent—and Lesueur *is* my bread and butter."

Wright looked sideways through the window at the shop-fronts of Fellaby High Street. Kenworthy would make a better job of it than this—

"And don't worry about Lesueur," the colonel said. "He'll come round. He always does. His bark's much worse than his bite. I'll have a quiet word with him."

He dropped Wright at the Report Centre. There was a telephone message from Scotland Yard. Heather had reported that Fischer of Siebenhausen was in gaol in Hamburg, halfway through ten years for receiving.

Wright returned to the hotel and set his alarm-clock to give himself an hour and a half's sleep.

· 11 ·

KENWORTHY WAS STILL not back. Wright debated with himself whether he ought to go and take a back seat at the settlement between the warring gangs. Strictly speaking, it was none of his business. Grayling was conducting the operation himself. He would not want the battlefield cluttered up with gratuitous spectators, and the score would be chalked up in the Congregational Sunday School as soon as it was known.

Nevertheless, as eight o'clock approached, Wright could not resist the temptation. His rest had left him, if anything, feeling worse than before, with the muscles of his neck stiff and every inch of his body calling out for cool pillow and sheets. But he made his way along the High Street, and opposite the *Saracen's Head* found the news-vendor in his favourite doorway.

"A lot of you boys out tonight."

"Yes. You may have missed the main show this morning, but you've got a ring-side seat for this performance."

"I see Grayling's out himself. Sitting in his car up Angel Street. This still to do with Barson?"

"Might be. Barson's goings-on spread over quite some territory."

"You don't have to tell me.—I see Dickie Watson's joined the plain-clothes mob. He was at school with me."

"So was Barson, you told me."

"Bloody bastard."

"You said you'd tell me."

"And I will. You can see how it is with me—"

He shook his left leg, which was withered to about a third

of its proper size, and hung back to front in his trouser leg. There was something wrong with his mouth, too, for his lower lip bulged forward like a pouch, and he had trouble with his saliva.

"Bloody living miscarriage, that's what I am.—All right, sergeant, I know the truth, I've looked in a mirror. Spare me your pity, that's all I ask. You can be sure I got none from that sod Barson. The other kids—well—you don't expect the milk of human kindness in a school playground, do you? But by and large they'd give you a hand when you needed it, even a bit of the core, when they'd finished with an apple. Not Barson. He thought I was funny. Got the others dancing round me, up against the railings, shouting and laughing. I never forgot it. I haven't forgotten yet."

"How old would you be when that happened?"

"How old? Stone the crows! Seven, ten, twelve, fourteen? It wasn't only the railings, and it wasn't only the playground. It was all the time, man. In class, when the teacher wasn't looking. On the recreation ground. Bonfire night—"

"All of which means that even if you knew who'd killed Barson, you wouldn't be so keen on telling me."

"That depends, doesn't it? It depends on who did do it. I don't make rules for myself. Too many other people doing that for me."

"I don't even know your name," Wright said.

"They call me Lenny."

Wright put his hand in his pocket to overpay for another paper.

"No need for that," Lenny said, "unless, of course, you can claim it on your expenses. I'm enjoying this. I never have to stir from here. Everything comes to me."

Wright brought out half a crown. Lenny put it in his pocket. Wright looked out into the deserted street. The sodium lights bathed pavement and road in an unnatural yellowness. The shop windows were all lit up: prams and babies' baths and pyramids of detergent packets.

"They're coming!" Lenny said suddenly.

On the opposite pavement, coming from out of town, Chick was approaching with long, gangling strides, leaning slightly forward as he walked, the fur coat shapeless on his shoulders, its sleeves too long for his arms. Beside him, barely keeping up with his pace, was the lieutenant in the bottle-green uniform with the gun-metal buttons. They turned into the *Saracen's Head*.

"We shall see something in a minute."

Almost immediately there was a roar of motor-cycle engines. They came from the same direction as Chick, in droves, on mopeds, two-strokes, 500 c.c. Nortons, some ridden solo, others with girls or side-kicks on the pillions. There were riders in crash-helmets and riders without; leather jackets plastered with brass studs in tawdry patterns, broad backs with their owners' names daubed in white paint: Mike, Red and Junkie. They came to rest at the kerb on both sides of the street, commanding the entrance to the pub, some of them wheeling round in the middle of the road, in contempt of an oncoming car. This would be Webbe's gang, the out-of-town bunch, the patrons of Sal's café.

Before the last of the engines had spluttered to silence, the uniformed police were out, from doorways, back alleys, side-streets, almost a constable to each machine, notebooks out, patient, plodding voices asking for licences and certificates of insurance. A dog-handler, with a black, bristling Dobermann Pinscher bitch had appeared from nowhere and was standing idly by.

Girls disentangled themselves irritably from pillions. A couple stood helplessly by whilst a policeman on a scooter far too small for him took it up the road to test its brakes. Wright heard off phrases reeled out in flat, parrot-like tones.

"Not fitted with an efficient warning instrument—ought to do something about the angle of this mirror, son—not expecting to be overtaken by aircraft, now, are you?—This pannier-frame's loose; hit a pothole and you'll have the bracket in your spokes, then where are you?—Ah, yes—you're the one who did the U-turn in front of the Triumph Herald, aren't you? Sorry, I shall have to report that.—If you'll tell me at which police-station you choose to report, within five days—"

There was no trouble. They were simply outflanked. Within fifteen minutes they had all gone, the way they had come, some of them wheeling machines which they dared not mount again. The police-car drove slowly back towards the town centre. The Dobermann Pinscher had unobtrusively vanished.

"That ought to help the poor tax-payer," Lenny said. "Two or three hundred quid in fines there, I shouldn't wonder."

Silence took possession of the street again and lasted about five minutes. Then the others began to arrive, in knots and groups, taking up positions of tactical prominence again, most of the newcomers on foot, but one or two on motor-cycles, one of which was left with its engine racing, almost outside Wright's doorway. The only diversion was from an undersized middle-aged mother, who came ploughing fearlessly through the crowd, clawing at a youngster's belt with the handle of her umbrella.

"You come on out of this! I'm not having you messing about with the Mods and Cons. You wait till I tell your father!"

This time, the police were not going to interfere. It was clever, Wright thought. The new leader of the Stanways gang had been elected by Grayling.

A group of eight youths bore down on the *Saracen's Head*, led by a tall, slender, physically immature youngster with long, thin arms and legs, like those of some exotic spider.

"I know him," Lenny said. "His name's Riley. Real young hellion!"

They entered the pub. A silence fell on all the groups. All eyes were focused on the doorway opposite. Some one came up and turned off the engine of the roaring motor-cycle.

There was an interval of about five minutes, then Riley came swaggering out of the pub, followed by his henchmen. He was wearing the fur coat, which looked grotesque on his emaciated frame. Gun-metal buttons came a yard or two behind him, not acknowledged by them, but following them back to town.

"So the borough has yet another new alderman," Wright said. "Do you reckon they beat Chick up?"

"Him? No! Chick Stanway? They wouldn't have to raise their fists. He'd start unbuttoning his coat the moment they came through the doorway. They'd just stay long enough for him to buy them all a drink. Now if it had been the other lot, there'd have been bloody noses for the sake of bloody noses."

Grayling had played it very shrewdly.

The hangers-on began to drift back towards the town. The last of them had gone before Chick came down the two steps of the *Saracen's Head*. He stood still for a few seconds, then belted his chest a couple of times with his arms, as if he were cold now that he had only his roll-necked jersey and his leather jerkin between him and the elements. He began to saunter back, the way he had come, away from the heart of Fellaby. Putty came out of the narrow passage between two shops. He did not see her at first, and then they seemed to argue. The she took his arm and they walked slowly out of sight.

· 12 ·

KENWORTHY WAS BACK at the County and dining alone, a
newspaper folded beside his plate. Wright sat down opposite him.

"Eaten, sergeant?"

"No—and I couldn't stand a full meal tonight. I'll have a
snack before I turn in."

There was something different about Kenworthy. He did
not want to talk, he did not want to listen, his face seemed
to have lost its colour.

"There was a message for you at the desk. I took it. Ring
up Lesueur. He wants to talk to you tonight. After that,
come up to my bedroom. There's a lot I want to get off my
chest."

There was cigarette-ash in the mouthpiece of the telephone, and Wright could not at first find the light switch of
the booth. Lesueur was hearty, and punctuated his mono-
logue with bursts of artificial laughter.

"Listen, sergeant, I'm sorry about this afternoon. Got to
apologise. Shouldn't have talked the way I did. Might have
had you thinking all kinds of wrong things. Ha, ha! Might
have had you thinking I'd got something to hide, ha, ha, ha!
Trouble is, I thought a hell of a lot of Edward. Can't bear to
think of all this under-linen having to be pegged out in
Fellaby. Still, I know you've got your job to do, all kinds of
unpleasant enquiries to make. Just as bad for you as it is for
us, really, I suppose. Only we don't naturally think of it that
way. Still, I want you to know, anything I can tell you, at
your service. Don't give another thought to what I said this
afternoon. Tell you the truth, funeral got me down this

morning. And I'll tell you what, I'm having the Chief Constable to dinner, day after tomorrow. Like you and Kenworthy to come. Good chance for a pow-wow."

Wright extemporised. He would have to ask the superintendent.

"Yes, of course, I know that. And if you have to call it off at the last minute, duty-wise, not to worry. All the more for the rest of us to eat. Ha, ha!—night, sergeant."

Kenworthy had not yet left the dining room. Wright went back to his table.

"I'll have a coffee with you, if I may. Though if I drink much more of the stuff, I don't know what it'll do to me. I'm getting palpitations already."

"Had a trying day, sergeant?"

"You might call it that."

"So have I. And I'm not going to talk about it here, in case of explosion."

They drained their cups without talking, Kenworthy lighting his pipe and letting it go out again.

"Come, Shiner!"

Wright looked at Kenworthy's bedroom as if he were taking part in an indecent invasion. There was so much of the intimate Kenworthy about—so many of the personal belongings of a superintendent that one did not normally see: Kenworthy's tooth-brush, in the rack over the wash-basin, Kenworthy's pyjamas on the bed, blue, faded, and definitely past their prime; a little stack of picture postcards of Bradcaster on a corner of the dressing-table, one of them written, stamped and ready for posting to Mrs. Kenworthy.

"Sit on the bed, Shiner. This is one mattress that you can't damage."

Kenworthy sat in the only chair and put a match to the bowl of his almost empty pipe.

"Shiner—I lost my temper today. And it's the first time that's happened to me since I held your rank. It's still got me rattled. I had a better opinion of myself. At one point, I must have come pretty near to wrecking my chances on this case, and in a man of my experience, that would have been unpardonable."

Wright neither interrupted nor tried to provide cues for further enlightenment. He waited through long seconds of silence, and then Kenworthy made a proper job of scraping out and recharging his pipe.

"Warren!" he said at last. "I'd better just remind you of the facts. Warren was chucked out of the Bradcaster City Borough Force three or four years ago. Chucked out winning, smiling all over his oily chops, knowing he'd pull some big brass down with him if they didn't let him out on his own terms."

Kenworthy's anger was not play-acted. He had met something he abhorred, and it had poisoned his system.

"Now he's set himself up in an office in Bradcaster's most expensive block. G Plan furniture and fitted carpets. High level tart in the ante-room with fingers like a vampire, who looks at you as if you're something not very savoury that she's just found inside a soused herring. And a two-way mirror, so that he can keep his beady little eyes on a battery of eight shorthand typists, battering away in another room as if he'd all the work on hand in northern England."

Kenworthy expended another match.

"Which I think he has. There's no doubting that Warren is booming. Divorce cases for the cream of the aristocracy and private information services to a member of the shadow cabinet. And he sees you in an office that hasn't got a scrap of paper in sight. Not a filing cabinet, not a calendar even. Just a nonsensical modern painting on a wall, about half an acre of polished desktop, and all the rest's nothing but arm-chairs, too bloody low to get out of, and bloody thousands of cut-grass ash-trays."

Having spent his main effort against Warren's furnishings, Kenworthy subsided.

"Supercilious sod, too," he said. "It gave master Warren one of the biggest kicks he's had for a long time, to be able to call his own tune to a yard man of my standing. He made it quite clear, without actually saying so, that we can't finish the Barson case without his help."

"And can we?"

"He could certainly cut a few corners for us, if he's a mind to. But I'm not buying anything off Warren—or begging it either. He was quite magnanimous, up to a point. Offered to make me a free gift of the file on Barson's garden. Also let fall a few gems of colourful information.

For example, although he doesn't have a seat on the board, and stays strictly in the background, your friend Lesueur has the controlling interest in *Futurco Publicity*."

"That's interesting."

"It's more than interesting. It slots a whole range of further suppositions into place."

"We should have come on to it before long," Wright said.

"Before long, yes. Warren's been working on this case much longer than we have. And his methods are slicker than ours. He can look at things we daren't ask to see. He's not responsible to anyone but himself. No protocol. No Judges' Rules. No regulations. And he's delved into this case very much more extensively than he cared to tell Gill. For example, he was careful to let it slip that he'd been out and about in Barson's working area, checking up on his contacts, calling at the hotels where Barson took his midday meals in the intervals between checking up on *Bisto* and *Guinness* posters.

"Again—we'd have got round to it," Wright said.

"In time. But remember—Warren didn't exactly have to count his pennies on this case. He could afford three quid to a receptionist or head waiter, where you and I would have had to account for five bob."

"And he didn't tell you what he'd found out?"

"He did not. And that, Shiner, is something that we've got to know about. I don't know whether Barson was a womaniser—"

"I've certainly drawn a major reaction three times when I mentioned his domestic background—to the town clerk, Lesueur and Hawley."

"I think I know why. I'll come to that in a minute. What worries me most is that Warren might still be in the game. It's certain that he found a good deal more in it than he ever proposed to share with Gill."

"You mean that even with Barson gone, there's still a chance of blackmail?"

"Obviously. It stands out a mile that there have been things going on in the Barson entourage that didn't start and finish with the parish pump—things that Barson couldn't have been handling without Lesueur. And Warren knows about them—but he hedged like hell, and I couldn't be certain why. That's what happens when you let yourself get rattled. You see, I knew he was playing it cool partly to humiliate me, and I've no doubt he thought that I'd be willing to pay at least a limited price for a neat conclusion. But I'm more inclined to think that his eye's really on the pile of pickings that's still in it for himself. It may well be something that he can afford to lie low about until the captains and the kings have departed. If we ever discover that Warren has called on Lesueur—"

"There is, of course, no evidence to suggest that Warren ever made a direct approach to Barson."

"Indeed there is not. I put that bluntly to Warren, and got as blunt a denial as I expected. That would make things too easy. It would, in fact, put me in a position of considerable danger."

Kenworthy stood up suddenly from his chair.

"If I thought there was a ghost of a chance of proving that Warren had accosted Barson, I wouldn't be able to see a single other tree in the forest. It would blinker me. And intricate though Warren's connection with this may be, there are plenty of other interesting characters who might have killed Barson."

He sat down again and laughed at himself.

"See how it's got me, Shiner? I hope you'll let this be a lesson to you."

"If Warren's crooked," Wright said, "he must be going to bed at least a trifle rattled himself tonight. There was a lot of bluff in his attitude to you. However much he may under-estimate us, he must know pretty realistically the line of thought you were following. You must have got him just a little worried."

"Oh, he doesn't under-estimate us, Shiner. He's got a very high opinion indeed of *me*. Damn it, he even offered me a job!"

Kenworthy got up and brought a hip flask from the flap in the lid of his suit-case.

"Go and get your tooth-glass, Shiner. We've both deserved sustenance. Then you can tell me how you've whiled away the day."

Kenworthy listened attentively whilst Wright recounted

his interview with the town clerk, his impressions of the
funeral, the story of Barson's crimes in Germany, the
progress reports from Heather, the conversations with
Lesueur, Hawley and Lenny, and the displacement of
Chick. Kenworthy made only monosyllabic interruptions.
When Wright had finished, he poured out more whisky.

"Let's come back to this reluctance of certain people to
talk about Barson's home relationships. I'm sure they're all
thinking of the same thing. That was why I didn't put you
in the picture earlier—why I was anxious for you to ask the
question in all innocence. I wanted an independent reaction,
and your own unprejudiced feeling about it. You see, we
think that Lesueur obliged with a passing squire act on
Hagley Brow in the late nineteen twenties. We think that
Barson's widow is Lesueur's bastard. We think—"

"When you say *we*, superintendent—is this the plural of
majesty, or—"

"Putty and I," Kenworthy said simply. "We think it all
fits in, you see. Barson was a nonentity when he first came
out of the army. Still pedalling round the remote hamlets
collecting two-pence per person per week. It wasn't until he
announced his engagement to Enid Sawyer, on his twenty-
first birthday, that things began to move. He was suddenly
encouraged to take an active interest in politics, found a safe
seat, given a worthless job at a preposterously high salary
that gave him all the time in the world to play the high and
mighty. I think that once Lesueur had shut the mother's
mouth he didn't give two hoots about the kid, until he saw
this chance to elevate her a little—though Putty says there
was always that bit extra at number 19 at Christmas, that
none of the neighbours could afford."

"Did Warren know this story?"

"Undoubtedly. But he said not a word to me about
it—which may in itself be significant. I'm sure he's a stage
ahead of us: he'll know whether it's rumour or fact. I'd give
anything to know whether he did any of his evangelising on
Hagley Brow. The questionnaires have drawn a stone cold
blank up there."

Wright splashed tap water into his whisky.

"I think," he said, "if you don't want me to get

absolutely lost in this case, you've have to let me in on a lot more of the things you've been learning from—Putty—"

"There you are, Shiner—you still don't like saying the word, do you? There must be something innately pure and lovely about you. Oh—she's a treasure, is our Putty. And all out of one cherry brandy, too. Don't you think you ought to go to bed, boy?"

"I want to hear more about Putty."

Kenworthy laughed.

"She's a mine of information about what goes on up Hagley Brow. She presents the figure of Sir Howard Lesueur as something almost feudal. In fact, I do believe that's what she thinks he is. Lesueur certainly believes it. In his relationships with his tenants, he's as feudal as the twentieth century will allow him to be. He owns the long lease of practically all the slum property on that side of the town—and that reminds me. We must tap the town clerk about this, tomorrow morning: a fair acreage of it was condemned and demolished a couple of years back, and I'd love to know what Lesueur's reaction was."

He rolled a drop of whisky round the tip of his tongue.

"Not that Lesueur's attitude is necessarily oppressive. He likes to play the beaming landlord now and then. Two weeks' free rent at Christmas for every tenant who hasn't run into arrears in the course of the year, and free access to the woods on the Fellaby Moor Estate to collect brush-wood for kindling. Very conscious of *noblesse oblige* is Sir Howard—when it suits his book. Of course, he doesn't go round the tenements himself—or very rarely. Rent-collectors do the weekly round, and anything out of the ordinary is done by Bill Hawley, in the gaps between running election campaigns and the Hall Estate. They think very highly of the colonel, up the brow."

"The Barman here had a good word to say for him. *I* liked him."

"It certainly seems to be Hawley's job to temper Lesueur's wind to the shorn lambs up the Brow. Many a tenant's been tided past an eviction. Lesueur's the big bad giant. Hawley irons out the troubles. I don't think it's as ingenuous as it seems. I think every move's worked out, and the pair work as a perfect team."

"He's certainly ironed things out for me. That's why we're going to dinner."

"Well, saving Lesueur's face is Hawley's main job.— And there you have it, Shiner. Putty knows it all. She also knows who's pregnant, who's behind with the milk, and who's making the most of who else's night-shift."

Wright rinsed out his glass. It was already after eleven o'clock. He had lost every chance of getting a meal in Fellaby that night. He began to fear that an empty belly would compete with his tiredness and that he was already committed to another sleepless night. But he remembered a machine which dispensed chocolate in one of the corridors of the hotel, and, wishing Kenworthy good-night, he made his way to it. But the column that had contained chocolate bars was empty and he had to settle for a tube of round, wrapped, viscous toffees. He took one as he slid into bed, and it was still half dissolved in his mouth when he awoke for breakfast.

He was late. He was late in the dining room, and so was Kenworthy. The two looked at each other with expressions that needed no expansion.

"We'll stick together today," Kenworthy said. "At least, we'll try to. We've worked our fingers to the bone already, and we're still no nearer to the end of the tunnel. Some cases are like this. I've never been able to learn to enjoy them."

He told the briefing conference about his interview with Warren, but suppressed most of the details about Warren's arrogance, and though he suggested that Warren might have found grounds for blackmailing Barson, he was careful not to link Lesueur's name with any speculation. He made it clear to an unspoken question asked by many eyes that Warren was not to be detained, as things stood at the moment; and no one except Kenworthy was to approach him. The press could now be told that the man in the green hat had come forward of his own accord, had been questioned at length, and that he was in no way connected with the towpath murder.

"Use that phrase. Give the public a new name for the case. Get the green hat out of their minds. But press on like hell with the questionnaires. No matter what other blanks we've drawn, press on with the questionnaires."

Rhys sounded as if he might be on the verge of becoming argumentative.

"These questionnaires—there are hardly any more to come in. And a full analysis of those we've done is available—"

Kenworthy had hardly looked at it.

"I know. But the computer doesn't say he went anywhere on Hagley Brow. That's what I want someone to come up with—Warren paying a call on Hagley Brow."

Rhys looked as if he were being asked to interview a creature from outer space.

"Superintendent Kenworthy—we've visited every house on Hagley Brow."

"Well, visit them again. Some of them, anyway. You must know one or two families up there who would react to a little sensitive suggestion."

"Very good, superintendent."

"And I want some one working out in the county—a couple of pairs—going over the territory that Barson used to cover for his firm. I'll brief these officers personally, when we adjourn."

Two sergeants and two detective constables were told off for this assignment, and they gathered round Kenworthy when the main body had been dismissed. There was an eagerness in their eyes which Wright recognized as fast disappearing from his own make-up. They were young, they were keen, they were being singled out for something out of the ordinary. They were doing finger-tip work for the mighty Kenworthy.

Kenworthy took them over to the wall map and divided the county into segments, each dominated by a small town.

"The man on whose heels you'll be treading is Warren. I needn't remind you that this calls for the last reserve of tact. You might even run into Warren himself, or one of his agents, in which case, you say not a word, not a blind word. Warren's been over this area, and built up a dossier on Barson. I want you to do the same. Barson's friends, Barson's habits, Barson's fancy bits. Go to restaurants, barmaids, betting shops, anywhere."

"Are we covered in other forces' areas, sir?"

"Rhys will get clearance for you. Work hand in glove with local nicks, where you feel it might help. If you get a line, follow it up. I don't want to be bothered over trivial detail, but if you strike anything that obviously needs more weight than you carry, then lose no time in coming back to say so. You're all experienced men, you know what I mean. I don't necessarily expect big results today, though I should like them. I shall certainly want brief reports tonight—any time tonight. Understand?"

The girl who had typed Wright's statement about the Bad Siebenhausen crimes came up and handed him the finished product. Malpas came up to say he had done as much as needed to be done on the borough falsification charges.

"Straightforward, really. And the quantity surveyor has coughed, so there's no need for a clutch of statements."

"Any sign of ramifications?"

"What sort of ramifications?"

"Any similar ploys? Any other councillors involved? Any offer of similar favours to members of the general public?"

"Anything like that wouldn't have been easily apparent. I only went into it as a single isolated case. Nobody said anything to me about ramifications."

"What system did they use to cover up the stock they were filching?"

"They had created a reserve supply by writing off as unserviceable material received from the wholesalers. A certain percentage margin would go unquestioned."

"Yes," Kenworthy said. "I once heard of a similar fiddle being worked with army transport."

"Anything further for me, superintendent?"

"I don't think so, inspector."

"I mean, now this case is tidied up, I'm free for any other angle you'd like me to cover."

"I'm sure your chief superintendent will be glad to feel that his own C.I.D. can now have your undivided attention."

Malpas left them with his shoulders sunk in dudgeon.

"Nobody said anything to him about ramifications!" Kenworthy snorted. "That'll teach him to come the acid on my sergeant when we ask for a second look at a broken window. Come—let's go and see the town clerk."

Belfield received them with a sigh, a smile and a dramatic sweeping aside of papers relating to other work.

"At least I have to thank you gentlemen for an astringent influence on my staff. Things are coming up for my signature that I wouldn't have set eyes on last week.—Or is this simply going to stifle all initiative?"

"They'll settle down to normality soon enough.—It's Sir Howard Lesueur we want to talk to you about. Not a friend of yours, I believe?"

The town clerk looked thoughtfully at Wright, but now that Kenworthy was present, he showed no reluctance to express his opinions.

"What does he do?" Kenworthy asked.

"I told you yesterday—shapes the whisper of the council chamber."

"I mean—where does his money come from?"

"From his money," the town clerk said.

"You mean, he inherited it?"

"No. He's self-made. I don't know much about his beginnings. They weren't in Fellaby. There's something of the nineteenth century novel about him, I'm told. As a very young man he became a faithful partner to a very old one. When the very old one died, he left him a decrepit but viable business. They were accountants—audited company books and gave advice on tax evasion."

"Is that his main line now?"

"Only on his own account. He hasn't touched public accountancy for years—not in the memory of anyone who knows him in this town. Nowadays it's anything and everything—anything that will pay, with an uncanny knack of anticipating markets by a year or two. The man has had consistent luck, as well as judgment—but that's not to deny that he has judgment."

"And the knighthood?"

"For political services—perhaps supported by very handsome contributions to party funds over a very long period of time. But please don't let me insinuate that he hasn't given service. He kept his party embers smouldering here throughout the depression. Two consecutive lord lieutenants have leaned very heavily on him. He is said to have known where to spend his money during a royal visit. And, of course, he's given a tremendous amount away: a new surgical unit to the Fellaby hospital. Four fifths of the war memorial."

"He told me he'd given you your museum," Wright said.

"Given? Saddled us with its upkeep, you mean! No, sergeant, Lesueur has too much business acumen for that. One day that property's due for development under the town plan. It'll have to come down. And when that day dawns, it remains Sir Howard's to sell. You can't afford to give unless you're actually on the make."

"He rents out a lot of property in the town, I believe—on the Hagley side."

"And if you'd wanted to catch Lesueur with his guard down, you ought to have seen him at the Appeal, a year or two ago, when we managed a demolition order for a couple of acres of the worst of it. He brought up one of his tame architects to show what delectable property it was. That was after someone's gas-cooker had fallen through the kitchen floor into a cellar no one knew existed. Lesueur cut a very pathetic figure indeed, but the national press had no room for it, and the local papers played it down."

"Isn't it surprising that he's stopped at a knighthood? It can't be through lack of ambition or effort."

"A barony, you mean? I'm sure that many an Honours List has disappointed him. If these things can be bought— and I'm not saying they can—he's bought his way into the Lords three times over. But somehow, amongst the real party bosses, his nose doesn't seem to fit. I don't know where the blockage is, but there's something somewhere. Politically, Lesueur is local fry—big local fry—but that seems to be his ceiling."

Kenworthy rubbed his lips with the stem of his pipe. Wright was taking copious notes.

"Now if I were to ask you, town clerk, what undertakings Lesueur is concerned in at the present time—?"

"I'd say that you've got your own channels, which can tell you very much more than I can. But you would have to glean your information from a variety of sources. Lesueur is a strong believer in the incompatibility of right hand and left."

"You could mention a few."

"Lesueur keeps his own tally. I should think he's lodged two halves of his will with two separate solicitors."

"A few," Kenworthy repeated.

"Whiteway Motors—that's a second-hand net-work on the coast; Kestrel unit Trusts; he has a controlling interest in Herbison, Son and Lever, the estate agents; he made a packet in I.T.V. in the early stages; Trefoil Breweries. Those are some of the ones we know about—probably the least important."

"Did you know that he is the power behind the firm that employed Barson?"

"I didn't—but it doesn't surprise me. I know he isn't on the board of directors. I remember looking, when Barson wrote to me once on the firm's note-paper."

"The board is just a front. He has the majority holding."

"This is one of his favourite ways of acting. He is fond of majority holdings and false fronts. He has propped up a number of decaying businesses in that way—and always at the turn of the tide."

"And where does Colonel Hawley come into all this?"

"He is his chief of staff—politically and on the estate. If he interests himself on the commercial side, it's not apparent. I dare say he has some substantial investments."

"What sort of colonel?"

"Lieutenant-colonel. He was a sapper major, who retired with honorary rank. He passed staff college as a career officer, was G2 at 8th Army and survived Montgomery, so I've always assumed that he was not without ability."

"How long has he been Lesueur's factotum?"

"Since between the wars, and ever since the last one."

"People seem to like him."

"He is a genial type—and he has often cushioned off some of Lesueur's more savage blows. He has always been adept at keeping both sides sweet. That's his job, of course."

"Would he talk about Lesueur, do you think?"

"Behind his back? Definitely not. Jocularly, perhaps, but

certainly not factually. Mind you, he did once have a stand-up row with Lesueur."

"Oh?"

"Over the Appeals Tribunal that I mentioned just now. Hawley had to give evidence about the Hagley slums. I won't go so far as to say that he told the whole truth—but he didn't tell any blatant lies. In my view it was Hawley who lost Lesueur's case for him. Lesueur was livid."

"But they made it up?"

"Yes—because Lesueur couldn't cope without him. And it was rumoured that Hawley got a salary rise before he withdrew his resignation. In any case, he'd taken the long-sighted view. If Lesueur had won that Appeal, he'd have lost what bit of affection he can command."

Kenworthy indicated the piles of papers awaiting attention on the town clerk's desk.

"I'm well aware that we are robbing you of the lion's share of a morning's work."

"I've done no real work this week. The sooner you've gone back to London, the sooner I can start again."

"It was Barson's job to interpret Lesueur's will to his party group on your council?"

"For what that is worth. I believe that it was no more than a craving for control—or, to put it negatively, the inability to tolerate not being in control. There was no money in borough council business for Lesueur—not Lesueur's kind of money."

"Not in any aspect of council affairs?"

"I cannot see it."

Kenworthy leaned forward, adamant.

"If there were anything in it for Lesueur, it would lie, would it not, in the sphere of redevelopment?"

"Possibly."

"And the prizes in that sphere would make it well worth while planning and waiting, play-acting and mayor-making, perhaps over a considerable period of years?"

"Possibly."

"Mr. Belfield—what schemes for redevelopment are pending in this borough?"

"Nothing for three years."

"But if something is going to happen in three years' time,

the crucial period for a forward planner is already wearing thin."

"There has been abundant speculation."

"And some broad decisions must already have been made."

"Very broad decisions."

"But enough to show which way the cat is going to jump?"

"In the confidence of committee. Nothing has yet been ratified in open council."

"I know you think I'm elevating this to a plane of fantasy," Kenworthy said, "and I know I'm putting an unfair strain on your code of professional etiquette, but I wish you could see your way to being more precise."

The town clerk pressed a bell-push.

"Shall we have coffee, gentlemen? I am not trying to break the thread of your very shrewd argument, but I think we could all do with a breather. Then I will tell you all you need to know on this issue. But it will not fit in with your thesis. The only way in which Lesueur could make money out of our redevelopment plans would have been in a manner which conflicted with the interests of his most influential supporters in this town."

Coffee was brought by a middle-aged woman in a dark skirt, white blouse and tie that might have been a school uniform. Wright remembered Kenworthy's description of Warren's receptionist, and this employee seemed to symbolise the mellowed woodwork and sober nineteenth century corridors of Fellaby town hall. And yet here, from these dusty box-files and the town clerk's heavy wooden out-tray, were proceeding plans to bring the town vitally into the heart of the times.

When they were left alone again, and Wright's digestive biscuit was crumbling in his saucer, the town clerk abandoned the wary mood which had marked the last few minutes, and appeared to be taking them more openly into his confidence.

"In three years' time, some of the borough's most valuable leases will fall in. They cover almost three quarters of the property on the south side of the High Street. And it will have to come down. It will be the last act I perform for

Fellaby before my retirement, and I propose to leave the town with a decent centre."

He leaned back in his chair, tired, proud and doggedly determined.

"Naturally, there are some forces which would like to preserve the *status quo*, but I think the current of operative opinion is safely won over. The Chamber of Commerce, which represents the town's trading interests—and, of course, the bulk of Tory money within Fellaby—favours a vast new civic centre, built over an arcade of shops to protect the interests of those who would otherwise be displaced. Lesueur could benefit in a small way from this—as an estate agent, backing builders, and so on. But this would be chicken-feed compared to what he could expect to make through a massive block of supermarkets and chain stores—which Fellaby does indeed lack. I know this is his intention, because the line Barson has been taking in committee is that we can no longer afford to look upon ourselves as a nation of small shop-keepers. Top class mass produced goods, at competitive prices, are the true requirements of the twentieth century customer. Who would buy his socks at Danny Farrow's prices, when he could save money elsewhere? I can assure you, the undercurrents have been turbulent."

"And Lesueur's money is in the supermarkets?"

"Obviously. It must be. That's the way his mind has worked since he invested his first thousand pounds."

"And if Labour win control?"

"I don't know. They'd like a new C.W.S. Emporium. I don't know whether they'd get it. *Please*," the town clerk said, "don't let me communicate a cynical attitude to local politics. I have seen so much of it that perhaps I am beginning to turn sour. But they're not such a bad lot. Barson—well, he was a nasty bit of work—"

He was evidently prompted by bitter personal feeling.

"And Lesueur is no more honest than any other wealthy man. But you mustn't interpret him as characteristic of his party. He doesn't always get his own way. Most of the Tories on this council are decent folk, desperately anxious to be just. Oh they like their little ration of dignity, but that's not a crime against society. They do what they think's right, and sometimes get hot under the collar about it. It's the same with the socialists. Durkin's ignorance is matchless, but he's an honest man. Some of his friends are still fighting battles that were won fifty years ago. But, God knows, those battles had to be fought. You've only got to look at the death-throes of Hagley Brow to realise that. But for the rest, they are men and women of integrity. They have their principles, and they stick to them."

Kenworthy changed the subject with dramatic suddenness.

"Do you really believe that Barson's wife was born on the wrong side of the blanket?" he asked.

"I refuse to trade in gossip," the town clerk said, "and I mean that."

· 13 ·

KENWORTHY SAT AT his green metal desk, looking through questionnaires. A clerk brought Wright a sheaf of typescript.

It was the detailed list of the names and home addresses of Barson's barrack-mates at the time of the Siebenhausen enquiry. Wright started at the word *Fellaby* in the right hand column, but as his eyes shifted along the line, he saw that it was Edward James Barson, of 11 Kenilworth Street. Someone had gone to the enormous clerical extravagance of typing out the army numbers of each of the two hundred or so men. But there was no one else in the list from within fifty miles of Fellaby. It proved nothing, but it achieved some further degree of elimination.

"Let's go back to the Carlton Estate, Shiner—like dogs to our vomit. If you remember, there was another woman who went *misère ouvert* on Green Hat. She was crowded out by the Oxfan coffee party—"

They were driven out to the estate in a black Ford Zephyr; damn it—they *asked* Kenworthy whether he wanted transport!

"House is next door to Barson's," Kenworthy said, "so this is going to cause a bit of a flutter. Still—we mustn't let ourselves become too sensitive, otherwise they'll never make policemen of us—Mrs. Graveney," he said, as he pressed the illuminated bell-switch. "I wonder if he got her between the sheets, too?"

Muffled chime-bars sounded within. The moment Mrs. Graveney opened the door, it was apparent that she was no Mrs. Crispin. Tall, slim, her toneless yellow hair was pulled tight over her head and tied with dark blue bands into two short tufts that stuck out at an angle behind her. She was wearing a navy blue tunic dress with a long panel that hung down in front of her to accentuate rather than hide an advanced pregnancy. On the floor a four-year-old boy in dungarees was kneeling in a pile of scattered wooden blocks, playing with a toy breakdown lorry.

"Oh, but I didn't see this man. I put that on the form we had to fill in, and I said it again to the detective who came afterwards. You see, it was a Thursday, and I wouldn't be in. Thursday's always my day to go and see Grandma Graveney—we love going to see Grandma Graveney, don't we, my poppet?—You know, I think an awful lot of nonsense is talked about the in-law problem. Don't you agree? I look forward to my Thursday mornings, and so does Grandma Graveney."

She talked as might one who had been deprived of human society for some weeks.

"So I'm afraid I'm not going to be much use to you. Though of course if there's anything I *could* tell you—"

Kenworthy's feet were already well established among the child's bricks, so Wright presumed they would accept an invitation to stay.

"There are one or two bits of things you might be able to help to clear up for us."

"I hope you won't mind being asked into the living room. I've lit a fire in there and—"

The fire was, in fact, nearly out. She threw a hurried shovelful on to the shallow red ashes, which appeared to extinguish it altogether. In what appeared to be one movement she swept up a pile of household litter: an ironing board, a heap of finished linen, the remains of the boy's breakfast, a tangle of damp-dried underwear, two newspapers from the floor and a bottle of pills from the mantelpiece. With all this in her arms she swept away into the kitchen. The infant brought his toy to Kenworthy's knees and thrust the jib of the crane into the superintendent's face. A reedy cuckoo popped from his door and added elevenfold comment to the confusion. A large picture window looked out on to a pair of brick dustbins in an open brick shelter.

"I'm sorry if we look lived in, but you see, we are, rather."

She scooped up the child and swung him, crane and all, in a frightening arc that narrowly missed the imitation candelabra, and deposited him on a dining chair.

"Now Clive, just be a quiet little boy whilst the big gentlemen talk to Mummy about poor Mr. Barson."

"You must have known the Barsons pretty well, Mrs. Graveney."

"Well, you know, he lived a very busy life, and her own daily round didn't leave a lot of time for garden-fencing, what with Bring-and-Buy sales and collecting for National Savings, and Primrose League."

"Tell me, Mrs. Graveney—do you have much to do with the other women in this avenue?"

"With the coffee-club, you mean?—That's what my husband and I always call them—always in and out of each other's houses. No. For one thing, my husband won't let me. He says that if ever he came home from his tea and found me out of the house helping Mrs. Crispin to tear Mrs. Lowther to pieces, he'd divorce me immediately."

She suddenly caught sight of a family planning booklet, visible behind an ornamental beer-mug on the mantlepiece, leaped and snatched it away and hid it somewhere in the folds of her dress.

"Was Mrs. Barson a regular member of the coffee-club?"

"Mrs. Barson comes in here and cries," Clive said.

"I expect she turned to you for condolence," Kenworthy hastened to suggest, but she did not take advantage of the proffered escape-route.

"Oh, no—that was before this happened. I haven't really seen her since then, and I haven't wanted to push myself forward."

Then she seized the boy by the shoulder and trundled him from the room.

"Naughty Clive, to mind other people's business. Clive must go and play somewhere else."

"Won't he catch cold in there?" Kenworthy asked, when she had returned.

"Oh, no. It isn't cold really. I've put the electric fire on.

To tell you the truth, I just didn't want you to see in there. It's a bit untidy."

"What makes Mrs. Barson come to you and cry?"

"Oh—I shouldn't talk about it, really. It isn't fair. It's like going behind some one's back."

"It isn't the same thing as talking about her, Mrs. Graveney. It's answering questions."

"Oh, well, of course—you *are* asking questions, aren't you?"

"I am."

"And I suppose something terrible would happen to me if I refused to answer."

"Something shocking, Mrs. Graveney. I should have to put in my report that you had been unhelpful."

"Oh, but I wouldn't want to give that impression. Emphatically the contrary. It's just that it feels all wrong to be talking about Mr. Barson—"

"Mrs. Graveney, sergeant Wright and I have it on unimpeachable authority that Mr. Barson was a nasty bit of work."

"Oh, well, in that case—I do know that he often wasn't very nice to his wife."

"You mean, they used to fall out?"

"Well—worse than that, really."

"You mean, he was playing away from home?"

"Playing away from home?"

"Keeping company with other women."

"Oh, no—I don't know anything of that nature, Mr. Kenworthy. I mustn't leave you with any such impression. That wasn't what I was thinking at all."

"Mrs. Barson never showed any suspicion that her husband might have a mistress tucked away somewhere?"

"No. This is a great shock to me."

"Well—just make sure that it doesn't shock anyone else. If a word of this leaks out, it can only come from one source, and Mrs. Barson will have you for the juiciest slander action in the annals of Fellaby. And you won't be able to look to me for protection."

"Oh, Mr. Kenworthy—I assure you—"

She was flushed, confused. Wright thought that Kenworthy was being unnecessarily tough with her, but a few seconds later the superintendent became the kindly family man again.

"In other respects, Barson treated her badly?"

"It must have been pretty bad for her to come and weep to me about it. We hardly knew each other, the first time she came."

"He used to keep her short of money, perhaps?"

"He did, rather. She was always having to play off one tradesman against the other, holding the soft drinks or the fish off until next month. But it wasn't that."

"No?"

"No—it was, well, sort of personal things—intimate things."

Kenworthy waited, but she was too embarrassed.

"The sort of thing you'd only care to talk to another woman about?"

"That's right."

"Well—we could arrange for a woman police officer to talk to you. But it would cause too much of a stir if I were to bring her down here. And equally, if I asked you to call in at the station, it would be all over the town in no time. And yet I must get to the bottom of it—I must know whether this is something that might have affected his relationships with people outside the home.—Just try not to feel awkward about it, Mrs. Graveney. Sergeant Wright and I have families of our own. Did you get the impression that Barson was some sort of pervert?"

"Oh, no, nothing like that. The things he wanted her to do were normal enough, I suppose. It's just that he hadn't any respect for her. He demanded too much from her."

She picked up the poker and stuck it as a lever under the lifeless coal. A few strands of thick, blue smoke welled up from the mountain of black dust, hung still for a moment, then evaporated. The fire was dead.

"He wouldn't use things, either—not even a few weeks after their third."

"Isn't there a clinic in Fellaby?"

"He wouldn't let her go. He said that in his position he couldn't afford to have his private life blazoned about the town."

"She could easily have had a word with her own doctor."

"He didn't want her to do that, either, though last time she talked to me about it, she said she was going to. And he'd put her off these pill things by frightening her about the side-effects."

"Do you think Clive's all right?" Kenworthy asked. "He sounds abnormally quiet."

But before the boy could be brought back, the door-chimes rang again.

"It's for you, Mr. Kenworthy."

Their police driver told them that a call had come over the car radio.

"Superintendent Rhys said it was important, sir. Said I was to advise you straight away."

"What is it, constable?"

"They've discovered that Warren, sir, paid a call on Hagley Brow. At number 19—"

"Number 19! Barson's mother-in-law!—Shiner, we're in business!"

"Number 19 Hagley Brow, sir?"

"No. County Hotel. No point in rushing things, and I don't want to interfere with Mrs. Sawyer's dinner. Besides, this is one thing I shall tackle better on a full stomach."

• 14 •

UP HAGLEY BROW the houses climbed in steep, uneven terraces, fronting to stone slabs of a much earlier vintage than those in Barson's garden, many of them sunk in their beds, so that one was in constant danger of stubbing one's toes. The windows of number 19 were covered with narrow crossed strips of brown gummed paper, as if the precautions of the air-raid years had set a permanent fashion.

Kenworthy and Wright had not announced their visit; they did not know what kind of reception awaited them. Mrs. Sawyer had not come forward of her own accord. Rhys's detectives had extracted the information by unscrupulous pressure on a neighbour who had previously withheld his information out of sheer reluctance to co-operate with the police on any issue whatsoever. Exhaustive follow-up had not revealed that Warren had called anywhere else in the row.

Kenworthy told the constable to drive away and park the car in a vacant lot they had noticed lower down the slope. Then he raised the knocker, which, like the number-plates, the letter-box and the door-knob, had been vigorously brought up with polish every morning for many years.

Mrs. Sawyer came to the door with a walking-stick, a big-boned woman who had been handsome in her time, but who was now beginning to stoop and lose flesh. She was well dressed, in black, with white hair, neatly kept and fairly recently permed.

"Police? You found out, then?"

Kenworthy introduced themselves.

"You'd better come in. I've been expecting you."

A heavy curtain had been drawn within the front door, otherwise the room opened directly from the street. She led them in, halting once to rest a painful hip.

"Arthritis," she said over her shoulder.

Her vowel sounds were markedly those of the local dialect, but she spoke with natural precision, her speech a combination of ancient tap-roots and unaffected refinement. The room was small and over full with furniture, but redolent with cleanliness and polish. A thick hearth-rug, of multi-coloured wool clippings, seemed almost new. The television set was small, but modern and expensive. A portable radio receiver on a shelf was at least a quarter of a century old, but had probably been a luxury when it was new. A big coal fire was burning in an old-fashioned kitchen-range, with a boiler built in at one side and an oven at the other, the whole thing meticulously black-leaded. She half raised her stick to draw attention to the crosses of brown adhesive paper on the window.

"Stops folk looking in," she said. "One of the few good things that came out of the war. I'll make tea presently."

She picked up an enormous copper kettle from its hob and went and filled it, noisily, in what was apparently a small scullery at the back of the house.

Kenworthy forebore to rebuke her for having shown a nil return on her questionnaire. She, for her part, accepted the discovery of her deception with neither shame nor the need for explanations. Perhaps she had spent a life-time dealing with set-backs as they came.

"It'll be about that Mr. Warren that you've come to see me."

"He told you his name, then, did he?"

"He wouldn't have got in my house if he hadn't."

"I'm afraid you've had a long series of shocks, Mrs. Sawyer."

"I'm no stranger to them."

There had been a Mr. Sawyer, for he was shown in a family group, with Enid in the toddler stage, on her hands and knees, crawling away into long grass. It was not an artistic group, an enlargement from someone's not very expert handling of a box camera. Mrs. Sawyer had been brawny and upright in those days, not exactly a beauty, but

mature, proud, comely, ripe for the picking. Her husband
had been smaller, pale faced, sad looking, on holiday in a
white open-necked shirt and well pressed grey flannels.
Perhaps he had been impotent without knowing it, Wright
thought; perhaps he accepted his lot philosophically, cling-
ing to what was left to him, trying not to resent what he had
lost.

"What did Warren want to see you about, Mrs. Sawyer?"

"Edward Barson," she said simply.

"He was prodding you for information, was he—trying to
get hold of personal background, and that sort of thing?"

"He got nothing out of me, Mr. Kenworthy. I can keep
my lips more tightly sealed than most."

She was disinclined to unseal them now, still quietly
assessing the reason for their visit, probing their good-will.

"What excuses did he give for his curiosity?"

"I didn't ask him."

"But I know you must have been wondering why he was
here. He didn't try the old one about representing some
religious organisation?"

"He wouldn't have got past the door."

"What did he say he was doing, then? Making hire
purchase enquiries? Investigating an insurance proposal?"

"He was a private detective. He made no bones about it."

"Did he say who he was working for?"

"I took it for granted he was working for the other
side—for the Labour."

"Has this sort of thing happened before, then? Have you
had other callers like this?"

"Never. But it didn't surprise me."

"What didn't surprise you, Mrs. Sawyer? That his
political opponents should be making enquiries about your
son-in-law? Or that there might be something in his background worth enquiring about?"

"I'm not one for play-acting," she said. "Barson was no
good. You weren't long in Fellaby, I'm sure, before you
found that out for yourselves. There never was much good
came out of Kenilworth Street."

"No. I gather that his environment was not ideal."

"It was no harder than my Enid's—and she was worth
four of him."

"This is our impression, too."

"I'm glad to hear that. I'm glad they pay detectives who can use their eyes and ears."

"Wouldn't you put Warren in the same class?"

"As you?"

"No—as Barson?"

"Set a thief to catch a thief."

Wright was reminded that chief inspector Dunne had used the same phrase when talking of Barson's chairmanship of the juvenile panel, but that the suggestion had never been developed. He leaned forward.

"Mrs. Sawyer—did you know Edward Barson when he was a boy?"

"I knew *of* him. Everybody in Fellaby knew *of* him. But I never knew him. I wasn't likely to. We had our own sense of pride on Hagley Brow. I didn't meet him until he started courting my Enid. I was sorry she ever took up with him. I tried to tell her what he was, but you mustn't say too much. You have to let them make their own mistakes. And she was fed up with me, fed up with this house—"

"What sort of reputation had he as a boy?"

"A real young hell-hound. Plague of the town."

Kenworthy was leaning back, smiling a little, letting Wright take over the questioning for a few minutes.

"But what sort of thing did he do? Something a bit beyond the normal run of boyish pranks, I suppose, like apple-scrumping and so on?"

"There ain't any apples in Fellaby, Mrs. Wright."

"No—but you get my meaning—"

"He stole, he lied, he was destructive. And he always saw to it that others took the blame."

The kettle began to sing. She edged it half an inch nearer the flames.

"I'll go and get the pot."

"Could be!" Kenworthy said quietly, while she was out of the room. "Could be!"

"You mean Lesueur?"

Kenworthy nodded.

"She's proud, she's seen better days, she's well set up here. She's made a little palace of this hovel. She wouldn't have wanted anything bigger or better, and she's got enough savvy not to have pushed her luck by making embarrassing demands on him."

She came back carrying a loaded tray, unable to put her stick to the ground. Wright hurried to help her.

"You're lucky I've got half a cake left. Bought, I'm afraid. I don't do much of my own baking these days, my hands are so bad. But I don't think you'd tell the difference. They use butter and fresh eggs at Ashmore's."

When she had given them plates and cups, Kenworthy took up the questioning again, smoothly, but at a faster tempo.

"Mrs. Sawyer—have you seen much of the Barsons since they were married?"

"Less and less, as the years have gone by. Enid tried at first to get me to join in with their social set, but I soon scotched that."

"Enid, of course, continued to visit you up here?"

"About once a month, that's what it boiled down to in the end. What is it it says in the Bible?—'Therefore shall a man leave his father and his mother, and shall cleave unto his wife.'"

"Did Edward Barson come with her?"

"Perhaps just before Christmas, to bring me my present. This year it was sloppy blue bedroom slippers with blue rosettes on them. I put them away in a drawer and haven't looked at them since. Apart from that, I didn't set eyes on him from one year's end to the next. I'd had my own way of letting him know where he wasn't welcome."

"Mrs. Sawyer, I'm sure you had. But no doubt you went down to the Carlton estate from time to time?"

"Not if I could help it. Too many pairs of eyes prying to see what he'd married into. A Barson!—Still, I can only be sorry for her now. If she wants my company, she can have it. If she prefers to stay away, I'll not thrust myself upon her. I'm only thankful that she's been spared this new round of horror. Unless, that is, you people are going to rake it up and throw it at her—"

There was a short silence in the room. A coal fell sideways in the fire, and Mrs. Sawyer shaped it up again with the poker.

"What new horror is this you're speaking of, Mrs. Sawyer?"

"Why, this new bit of jiggery-pokery of Barson's," she said.

"There seem to be so many.—Which one in particular?"

"This woman. He was keeping a woman out at Kirby-le-Dale. At least, that's what Mr. Warren said."

"Warren told you that?"

"He did. I thought that was his main reason for coming to see me."

"We've been hoping to keep that side of the story out of Fellaby," Kenworthy said, without a flicker in his expression. "We'll still do our best.—Did Warren enlarge on the details?"

"Not a thing—and I wasn't interested."

"You don't know her name?"

"I couldn't care less."

"But you don't find it difficult to believe?"

"I don't find anything about Edward Barson hard to believe."

Kenworthy rubbed his hands as they walked down to where the car was parked.

"I said we were in business, Shiner."

"I'm afraid I don't get it," Wright said.

"Neither do I. And isn't this just what we wanted? Up to now everything has been just too plain and logical. There's not been a single discrepancy we could get our teeth into. You'll never get to the bottom of a case like this until you unearth something that obstinately refuses to fit."

"Why on earth should Warren go dropping a clanger like that up on Hagley Brow?"

"I haven't the foggiest idea, Shiner."

"It blows holes in any blackmail theory. A blackmailer cuts the ground from under his own feet if he reveals his story prematurely."

"He does indeed."

"And Warren's far too experienced an operator to foul his own nest."

"Indeed he is."

"He can't have done it just for the sake of working a mischief."

"I wouldn't have thought so."

"That wouldn't have helped either Gill's interests or his own."

"How right you are!"

"And yet I'm inclined," Wright said, "to believe everything that old woman Sawyer told us. The sole reason for his visit was to put this particular cat amongst the pigeons."

Kenworthy pushed open the door of the Zephyr.

"That is the crux of the problem to which we have to apply our intellects in the next few hours."

"He might have wanted to provoke the woman's husband," Wright persisted.

"What husband?"

"I expect she's a married woman."

"Bloody clairvoyance, now," Kenworthy muttered. "What advantage do you think he'd derive from provoking the woman's husband? The only advantage Warren ever seeks is material gain."

"Perhaps Warren was mixed up with this woman, too."

Kenworthy only grunted. Wright saw that he was not being exasperating for the sheer enjoyment of it; silently and furiously the superintendent was thinking. Wright held his peace.

Once they were back in the Report Centre, Kenworthy was on tenterhooks for news of the sergeants he had sent out into Barson's operational area. But they were in cars that were not equipped with radio, and there was no up-to-date news of them in any of the police stations that they might have visited.

Rhys came up and made another attempt to rid himself and his men of the burden of the questionnaires.

"No! For Pete's sake! Don't you see that those questionnaires have now trebled in importance? Any odd remark that Warren might have let slip on anyone's doorstep might tell us what we want to know. You can take the pitcher ninety-nine times to the well without breaking it. Visit some of these householders a fourth and fifth time, if it's necessary to jog their memories."

"Superintendent Kenworthy, I shall not refer to these questionnaires again in your presence until on your own initiative you tell me to abandon them."

"You can go on with them for thirty years after I've closed the case, if you like, as long as you come up with something in the next twelve hours."

It was early evening before the mobile sergeants returned. They had nothing to report.

"Have you done Kirby-le-Dale yet?"

"No, sir. Tomorrow morning."

"Tomorrow morning?—Tonight!—No, on second thoughts, make it tomorrow morning. If you go tonight, you'll have her husband on your shadows. And the pubs will be crowded tonight. Any questions you ask will stir up too much interest. Tomorrow morning, first thing, crack of dawn, my lad."

"Who is she?" a sergeant asked.

"How the hell do I know who she is? Do you think I'd be standing here, doing a Bones and Sambo act, if I knew who she was? Go and find out who she is, and when you've done that, go and find *her*. And when you've found her, I want her back here, as fast as a goose-dropping."

Rhys came and sat at his desk, flaunting an armful of duplicated pro formas. Kenworthy beckoned Wright out of the room.

"Let's have an evening off, Shiner."

"Putty, sir?"

"Alas, Shiner—I fear that the breach with Chick has now been healed. So I wouldn't stand a chance."

"A fat lot there is to do in Fellaby," Wright said.

"Go to the pictures."

"What's on? Al Jolson? I think chief inspector Dunne is night duty officer for the rest of the week. I'll go and chat him up."

"What the hell do you want to go and chat Dunne up for?"

"I think he can tell me more than he already has about Barson's boyhood."

"What are you thinking of doing Barson for now? Scrumping apples?"

"Perhaps I'll go and have another word with Lenny."

"Pity he doesn't flog his papers on the towpath. There's no telling what he might have seen."

Wright kicked the side of his foot against the kerb.

"Give it a rest, Shiner," Kenworthy said, "that's what I'm going to do. I'm going upstairs to write a couple of post-cards, and after that I'm going to an early bed. Take my mind off it. Give the jolly old sub-conscious time and chance to throw something up."

• 15 •

THE NEXT DAY dawned as one of those displaced precursors of spring that brought a new mildness to the air, a tingling of flesh, and expanses of blue sky above the slate roofs and television aerials of Fellaby.

Kenworthy insisted on taking Wright for a walk across the park. A gardener with a wheel-barrow was unchoking leaves from the grids of land-drains. A rook picked up a brittle black twig and flapped to an untidy nest at the top of a tree almost in the centre of the town.

"Isn't it tonight that we're sticking our snouts in the trough with Lesueur and the Chief Constable?"

"It is. I haven't confirmed it yet."

"Better do that. I can't think of anything that's likely to be more vital—or more informative. And when you've finished phoning, come back and join me here. I'm going to sit and enjoy this exquisite sunshine. We can see from here when the cars come back from Kirby-le-Dale."

When Wright came back, Kenworthy was sitting on a park bench with his newspaper on his knees. Within its folds he had his football pools coupon, on which he was filling in the Treble Chance.

"O.K., Shiner?"

"Yes."

"Nothing new?"

"No."

"Nothing in tone or subtlety?"

"No. I only spoke to Hawley. He seemed to know all about it."

Wright sat gazing at the lawn in front of him while

Kenworthy inserted X's in columns after periods of pro-
tracted thought.

"One of my biggest problems, Shiner, is knowing the
psychological moment to tackle Hawley. It's got to come,
and I've no doubt that it'll be a rewarding interview. But the
whole issue will be made or marred by the timing of it. If
Lesueur's as deeply involved as I think he might be, then
Hawley's the one man who might tip him the wink if we get
too dangerously near the penalty area."

"Does that necessarily follow, sir? If Hawley wouldn't
support his boss over the demolition of a couple of slum
streets, would he connive where murder's concerned?"

"Where murder's concerned, Shiner, it's fatal to lean too
heavily on logic. I inspired a bit of chatter about Hawley in
the County bar after I'd sent you to bed last night. He's well
thought of, and he's a clever man. And the cleverest thing
about him is the benevolent image. I don't deny that that
may be his natural temperament—but it's a useful instrument of policy, too. And it works like a charm.—Hullo!
Here they come!"

On the road which they overlooked, a dark blue Cortina
slowed for the corner. Kenworthy tapped Wright's knees
with his newspaper.

"Action, Shiner! But try not to look too eager!"

The plain-clothes men had put the woman in a sparsely
furnished interview room. A woman police sergeant was
sitting with her.

"Mrs. Monica Sturgess," she announced.

"Stay with us, please," Kenworthy said.

"I want my solicitor," the woman moaned.

"Don't play hard to get."

"I've always understood that a person under questioning
is entitled to a solicitor."

"We'll get him for you, then. But who's going to pay his
fee? Your old man?"

"You win.—But get on with it. If I'm not back in
Kirby-le-Dale by tea-time—"

"You could be. Depends largely on yourself.—One
question out of turn, before we start on track one: are you
working for Warren?"

She was in her late twenties, raven black hair swept to

one side and hanging over her right shoulder, translucent pale blue blouse cut low, exhibiting as much sex as the C.I.D. sergeant had given her time to deck out.

"Who's Warren?"

She was trying to assume an American nonchalance without extending herself as far as trans-Atlantic vowels.

"We'll come to that later. Name? Maiden name? Date of birth? Place of birth?"

"I'm sorry I left my school reports at home."

"We'll call for them if we need them. When did you first meet Barson?"

"About six months ago."

"How? Where?"

"He called to see my husband."

"Is *he* anybody?"

"Brian Forshaw Sturgess. Born 11th October, 1928. Brown eyes, dark wavy hair, small mole over the right nipple."

"What does he do for a living? If he's in the same line of business as Barson was, the answer is, not much."

"He's a company director."

"That's a common complaint. Whom does he direct, and in what direction?"

"Several companies—subsidiaries, holding companies. I don't know all the terminology. They're all in the same group."

"Do they trade anonymously?"

"*Salamander Enterprises.*"

"Sounds imposing. What do they actually do?"

"I don't know any details. I've no head for business. Brian doesn't discuss his work with me."

"But a clever girl like you must have formed some general impression."

"It's a trading group."

"Trading in what?"

"Anything they can lay their hands on."

"Wholesale? Retail?"

"Both. Cut out the middleman, that's their motto. Shave the overheads. Pass on the savings to the customer."

"Some of them, anyway, I suppose. Does his work take him away from home much?"

"Often."

"Helps, doesn't it?"

"Don't be such a bloody prig," she said.

"I'm not a prig. I said, it helps. Frequent trips away from home, which are often followed by substantial contributions to the household budget."

"Not that you'd notice."

Kenworthy pencilled a note and passed it to Wright.

Get Heather on to Salamander. Everything, including share-holders if possible.

When Wright came back into the interview room, the woman was pouting, Kenworthy was leaning forward with both wrists on the table, the woman sergeant was watching impassively.

"All right, Mrs. Sturgess. Adultery isn't a crime in this country. But an adulterous affair with a man just before he's murdered is a situation which makes me curious. And it's a situation which might put your husband in a very curious position indeed."

For the first time, she failed to cover her discomposure with bluster. This was a possibility that had simply not occurred to her.

"No, no. Brian didn't know. I'll swear it."

"Didn't Warren tell him?"

"No. I'll admit that Warren came to see me, but—"

"Did Warren threaten to kill him?"

"No. Nothing like that."

"Well—it's something to have got you to change your mind about knowing Warren. But let's continue to leave Warren out of it for the time being. We'll have plenty to say about him later. Let's hear first of all what you thought about Barson."

He looked at her expectantly. She did not know what to say.

"Come, Mrs. Sturgess. His character?"

"Character?"

"It is possible for a man to possess one, you know, Mrs. Sturgess."

"Well, he was gay, witty, knew his way about food and clothes. Powerful in his political circle, I think. Didn't suffer opposition gladly. Frustrated."

"Frustrated?"

"In his home life."

"You've not met his wife, Mrs. Sturgess?"

"Obviously not."

"Seen her photograph?"

"He didn't carry it with him."

"I suppose not. Well—let's recapitulate. Barson came to see your husband on business about six months ago. You took a liking to each other. He appreciated your particular gifts. Where did you start meeting?"

"There's a discreet little pub. A Free House. Up on the moors."

"And then he started visiting you at home?"

"He came once or twice to see Brian on business, but Brian was away."

"How often did he see you?"

"Oh—twice most weeks. Sometimes there were gaps— his work or Brian's."

"Where was all this going?"

"I don't know what you mean."

"Didn't Barson ever talk of getting a divorce?"

"Good God, no. He didn't want that."

"And didn't you?"

"Good God, no."

"You're perfectly happy with your husband?"

"Perfectly."

"Didn't Barson ever talk of making a lot of money and taking you away with him?"

"Only as a joke."

"This big pile that he was going to make—it had to do with the business he was conducting with your husband?"

Mrs. Sturgess tried to laugh.

"Men like Edward Barson and my husband are always on the verge of making a big pile. It never seems quite to come off."

"And you have no idea of the nature of this business?"

"He didn't discuss it with me. I wouldn't have understood, anyway."

"Was it concerned with Barson's work as an advertising executive?"

"I wouldn't know."

"Or had it something to do with Barson's activities as a Fellaby borough councillor?"

"Edward did say that he could bring a lot of Fellaby Borough business in Brian's direction."

"And yet a moment ago you said he had never discussed it with you. Mrs. Sturgess—do you appreciate how dangerous it is for you to be disingenuous with me?"

"I don't know what that word means."

"Bloody bent!" Kenworthy said, and thumped the table with his fist. She recoiled, and her fear showed through the surface again.

"I'd forgotten all about it until you mentioned it. I never really paid attention. Business talk always bores me stiff."

"But you must have gathered something about this particular business."

"They never went into detail in front of me. And Edward and I had other things to talk about."

"Was the word 'redevelopment' ever mentioned?"

"That was one of the things. I do remember that, now. Superintendent—I do ask you to believe me. All this is foreign to me. Brian never talks shop to me. He prefers to leave his work behind in the office."

"Try to remember some more."

"It was a question of who was going to benefit from wholesale rebuilding of the town centre. But how it was all going to work out, I haven't the slightest idea. You know how men are when they're talking about that sort of thing in the presence of a woman—like when they won't finish a dirty joke because you've just come into the room."

"Have you ever been in Fellaby before, Mrs. Sturgess?"

"Never in my life. What would anybody want to come to Fellaby for?"

"To commit a murder, amongst other possibilities. Had your husband ever been here?"

"Definitely not."

"What makes you so certain?"

"When Edward first mentioned the place, we had to get the map out to find out where it was."

"Perhaps he's been here since—to check up on the redevelopment possibilities."

"I'm sure he hasn't."

"You have a habit of feeling sure about certain important features."

"I know he hasn't been to Fellaby. He'd have told me. You see, Fellaby had become a sort of family joke at home. Country hicks, and all that."

"Did Barson ever mention the names of any Fellaby people?"

"If he did, I've forgotten them."

"Not even, perhaps, Lesueur?"

"That's right. I remember there was some one with a foreign-sounding name. And there was some one else—a colonel—"

"Hawley?"

"That's right. You know everything already, don't you, superintendent?"

He ignored these sporadic returns of ebullience.

"Lesueur and Hawley—what impression did you form of their role in all this?"

Wright looked sideways at the woman sergeant. This was the first firm suggestion that any member of the local force had had that Kenworthy was seriously linking Lesueur's name with the Barson case.

Her face was inscrutable, but it would not take long for an account of this interview to find its way to the ears of Rhys and Grayling. Presumably this was Kenworthy's intention.

"Where did Lesueur come into this?" he repeated.

"I guess he was the brains behind it."

"Only the brains?"

"And the money, I suppose."

"You heard some stories about Lesueur being a power in the land?"

"Edward said that he would make or break anyone who stood in his way."

"And the colonel?"

"Lesueur's right-hand man. Edward said that he was the one they had to watch. If the colonel cottoned on to what was happening, the game was up."

"And how might the colonel cotton onto things?"

"Well—Lesueur likes to play landed gentry. The colonel's less aloof. He gets around on the ground, as it were."

"Did it impress your husband, to have a chance to be working with Lesueur and Hawley?"

"Brian had never done business on that plane before."

"Then this was to be a major break-through for him?"

"Sort of."

"Elevenses," Kenworthy said. "You're not doing badly, Mrs. Sturgess. You've deserved a cuppa."

He let the woman sergeant go out to see about the coffee. Wright wondered whether this were a deliberate attempt on Kenworthy's part to start a rumour among the senior ranks of the station. Rhys would certainly be waiting to pounce on her.

Mrs. Sturgess stood up to stretch her limbs and went to the window that overlooked the transport park. She was not unattractive, Wright thought. Barson might have done worse for himself. And even now she was not averse to letting it be seen where her capital lay.

"Am I allowed to smoke?"

"Of course."

Kenworthy slid a packet of cigarettes across the table.

"Thank you. I prefer them tipped."

She opened her handbag. Wright went forward with his lighter. The woman sergeant brought in a tray.

"Now, Mrs. Sturgess—let us come on to Warren. How long since he came to see you?"

"Two or three weeks."

"What put him on to you?"

"The same thing as your men, I suppose—tittle-tattle."

"He must have had you pretty frightened, Mrs. Sturgess."

"Rigid. When he said he was a private enquiry agent, I thought at first he must be working for Mrs. Barson."

"He didn't try to trade on that?"

"No. Of course, he used it to get his foot in the door."

"He didn't try to ask you for money?"

"That would have been a laugh."

"Did he, or didn't he?"

"He didn't."

"Weren't you afraid that that might come later?"

"I was afraid of everything. I didn't know what to expect."

"He pumped you pretty hard about your relationship with Barson?"

"He went over it all, just as you've done. But he seemed to know the answers to all the questions before he asked them."

"Such as the pub on the moors, Barson's day for calling, and whatever?"

"He seemed to know everything. Not that it would have been hard for him to find out, in Kirby-le-Dale, once he'd got on the trail."

"And he didn't threaten to tell your husband?"

"No more than you have. He used it as a lever to find out what he wanted to know. In the end he promised faithfully he wouldn't say a word."

"In exchange for what—for favours received?"

"Mr. Kenworthy—I find that a bit cheap."

"I'm glad you think something is.—In exchange for what, Mrs. Sturgess?"

"He went on, just as you did, to talk about the deal Edward wanted Brian to do."

"And what did you tell him?"

"More or less what I've just told you."

"So that's twice in recent weeks that you've had your memory jogged?"

"Oh, can't you see, Mr. Kenworthy—I'm so lost in all this?"

"When in doubt, tell the truth. That's a maxim worth remembering for this kind of trouble."

"I've told you all I do know. And that's all I told Warren."

"And what aspects of it interested him most?"

"All of it, I think. But it was hard to tell. Even when it came to business, he seemed to know everything beforehand."

"Lesueur?"

"He knew all about that."

"And Colonel Hawley?"

"I don't remember that he mentioned him. He certainly didn't single him out."

"Who was the first to mention Lesueur's name—you or he?"

"I did.—Oh, Mr. Kenworthy—I know I was letting you take me along step by step. But I didn't want to look guilty. Can't you understand?"

"When you confirmed that Lesueur was the big name behind all this, did Warren look pleased?"

"Satisfied."

"That was the end of the interview?"

"That was all there was to it."

"He didn't say he would contact you again, or ask you to keep him posted with further information?"

"No. I was afraid he might come again, but he hasn't been."

Wright had come to the end of the notebook and was beginning to scribble on the inside cover. The woman sergeant passed him a small wad of plain quarto paper.

"Did you tell your husband about Warren's visit?"

"Of course not. What do you think?"

"You could have told him half the story—the business half."

"Brian would have found out where Warren's office was, and would have gone to see him. I've been dead scared from the moment Warren first appeared on my door-step. Wouldn't you have been?"

"I doubt whether I would ever have found myself in such a complex situation, Mrs. Sturgess.—What were your reactions when you read in the papers what had happened to Barson?"

"Well, of course, I was stunned."

"What did your husband say?"

"That there was another small fortune gone down the drain. Brian misses the chance of a small fortune on an average twice a month."

"Even the enormity of this murder didn't make you want to take your husband into your confidence?"

"I badly wanted to talk to someone. But I thought it was the best policy in the long run to keep my mouth shut."

"In a sense you must have been relieved."

"What are you suggesting, Mr. Kenworthy?"

"Nothing. Nothing at all, Mrs. Sturgess. The thought never entered my head."

Kenworthy put his tobacco pouch and matches back into

his pocket—a sign, Wright knew, that the interview was almost over.

"There's just one more question, Mrs. Sturgess—and you needn't answer it if you don't want to—was your husband using you as bait to hook Barson and Lesueur?"

"I could report you for saying a thing like that," she said.

Kenworthy turned to the police-woman.

"Tell her where she can get a spot of lunch in Fellaby, and then lay on transport to take her back to Kirby-le-Dale."

"Will that be all?" Mrs. Sturgess asked, uncertain of herself.

"Your guess is as good as mine—better, in fact, because you know the answer to some of the questions that I haven't asked."

And as her rear view disappeared down the stairs in the wake of her guide, superintendent Rhys came fortuitously from another office, clutching a dozen questionnaires in his hand. He looked in at the open door of the interview room.

"Something I ought to know about?" he asked brightly, without a trace of innuendo.

"Just been saving you a dollop of extra work. Eliminated a couple of suspects."

"Oh?"

The Welshman came into the room and closed the door behind himself.

"One of Barson's shadier business contacts," Kenworthy said, "and his wife, whom you've just seen. Barson has been playing around with her."

"Did the husband know?"

"We don't think so."

"But they've both got an alibi, I suppose?"

"As good as," Kenworthy said. "There are some aspects of any story that you know are fictitious, and some that have the hallmark of naïveté about them—a sort of unembroidered picturesqueness. In this case, it turns on the certainty that neither Sturgess nor his wife had previously set foot in Fellaby."

"They wouldn't have needed their feet in Fellaby for very long."

"But remember, superintendent—whoever killed Barson knew where he could put his hands on the Lugar—and armed himself with it the previous night. I'm sure beyond all shadow of doubt that that lets the Sturgesses out."

"Nevertheless—you'll be wanting us to follow up—as a precaution?"

"Later, Rhys.—Always give apples time to ripen, otherwise they'll give you a belly-ache."

Rhys took his questionnaires elsewhere.

"Just think of it, Shiner," Kenworthy said. "This is pure Lesueur. *Salamander Enterprises*—a small, multiple company that no one's heard of. Probably its finances are a bit anaemic, until Lesueur gives them a transfusion. Then Barson and his pals vote them a monopoly of the new High Street—Lesueur's happy, Barson's happy, the Fellaby shopper is happy."

"But why should they be afraid of Colonel Hawley? Why should the game be up if he rumbles what they're doing?"

"I'm not sure, Shiner. I think it's because as official party agent he'd want to keep the political lines uncrossed. I don't think Hawley cares much for gerrymandering. But I'm not sure. I think Mrs. Sturgess may have got two visits from Barson muddled up."

"I don't follow, sir."

"Think it out, Shiner—"

"Obviously we shall have to question Sturgess."

"All in good time, Shiner.—Sturgess didn't do it—of that you can be dead certain—for the reasons I gave to Rhys, and one other, which I didn't. Sturgess may have his usefulness to us—but it can wait. His adoring wife will make a clean breast of things—that's a nice bit of imagery, isn't it?—when he comes tonight. She'll have to. As she said—and it was one of the few bare bits of truth she came out with—she's lost in all this. And now it's sunk through her thick skull that her husband might be the number one suspect, she'll be more lost than ever. So Sturgess will come tumbling into our arms—if only to try to find out what we're thinking. If he were guilty, he wouldn't, but if he's innocent, he will. And he'll be dead scared, too. I only hope he won't come craving our attention too soon. I don't want to be confronted with him until I can argue with him from strength about *Salamander Enterprises*. Otherwise he might palm me off with half a story. But when I've digested the report that Heather will send us, he won't be able to palm me off with anything at all. This is the sort of thing that Heather does rather well—only it's bound to take him a bit of time."

"What now, then?" Wright asked.

"Din-din, Shiner. And let's save a few bob. Let's go down and nosh bangers and mash with the vulgar constabulary."

·16·

RHYS WAS DEMOLISHING a mountain of Irish stew at the next table. He was called away to the house-phone and went bounding up the lino-covered stairs. Kenworthy glanced sympathetically at the half-finished meal congealing on his plate.

"Who'd be a copper? Gives some men ulcers."

"Do you think it's something for us?"

Wright nodded towards the stairs.

"Sure to be. I dare say Rhys has given instructions at the switch-board that's he's to be given the first look at messages now and then. Some buggers you have to work with will try to hog everything."

It was twenty minutes before Rhys came back down the stairs, clattering with his feet and clearly in a high state of excitement. By now a tubby woman in a green overall coat and mob cap had come and carried away his plate of stew, looking askance at the great blobs of white fat that had formed on the gravy. But Rhys did not look at the table at which he had been sitting.

"Well, this seems to be it, superintendent. Three persons upstairs, waiting to make statements."

"Want me to come?"

"I should have thought—"

"Think I'll be interested?"

Rhys looked at him with bulging eyes.

"There are three persons upstairs who are asking to make statements which directly incriminate the murderer of alderman Barson."

"That's what I thought you meant.—Well, I'm not going

to let them give *me* indigestion. They've waited—how many days?—well, they can wait till I've finished my afters."

Kenworthy dug his spoon into a slab of date-pudding.

"I'll wait for you, then," Rhys said, hoping to be told to carry on alone.

"If you would, please.—Aren't you going to have some more to eat?—Well, have a coffee with us."

Kenworthy managed to extend the strain on Rhys's nerves for a full quarter of an hour. Then they went upstairs to the interview room, in which the young man in the drab artificial military uniform was waiting with a couple of other youths.

"This is Lawrence Yarwood," Rhys said. "He's volunteered the information that he heard Stanway making unambiguous threats to kill alderman Barson, and saying specifically that he proposed to use the Luger from the Borough Museum for the purpose."

Kenworthy looked at the youth with exaggerated distaste.

"Stand up!"

Yarwood obeyed quickly, but with no suggestion of military bearing.

"I've seen you before, haven't I—in the *Saracen's Head*."

"Yes."

"*Sir!*"

"Yes, sir."

"You were hand in glove with Stanway then, if I remember correctly."

"I knew him."

"You were his side-kick, I thought, his buddy, his number two, his right-hand man."

"I got out of it. Could see the way things was going. Who wants to be hand in glove with a bloody murderer?"

"So what have you got to tell us?"

"Like this other bloke says—"

"This other bloke happens to be a detective superintendent."

"Like the detective superintendent says. Chick said he was going to do Barson."

"I heard him with my own ears saying that he wished he had. Does this amount to the same story?"

Rhys stood watching and listening with increasing discomfort. This was the first he had heard of Kenworthy's visit to the *Saracen's Head*. Kenworthy's previous acquaintance with Yarwood was one of the most effective pieces of one-upmanship that Wright had ever witnessed.

"No sir, honest. This was before it happened, see? He said definitely he was *going* to do it."

"Kept it to yourself long enough, didn't you?"

Yarwood looked desperately over his shoulder at his friends.

"We was talking it over, see?"

One of the others spoke.

"Yeah—we reckoned he was bloody daft, see? A bit of fun's all right, on the bikes and what-not, but we didn't want nothing to do with no murder."

Kenworthy seemed to ignore him.

"Where is this conversation supposed to have taken place?" he asked Yarwood.

"Over in Wardle's."

"That's the name of the ramshackle building by the canal, where they've been having their meetings," Rhys explained, "and where the Luger was found."

"Were several of you present when he said this?"

"Yeah. We was most of us there that night."

"Did Putty hear it?"

"Yeah. She was always hanging around."

Wright dared to look at Rhys. The Welshman had set his jaw and was determined not to betray that he had not heard of Putty before.

"And Chick said, unambiguously and specifically—that means, bang to rights—that he was going to the museum to get the Luger to do it with?"

"Yeah. That's right. He'd always said he was going after that Luger. Wanted it for the gang, see? Not to use, get me, just as a sort of—well—mascot."

"Like the mayor's mace?"

"Dunno what you mean?"

"No. You wouldn't be versed in the finer points of civic ceremony. You ought to get yourself genned up, Yarwood.

You might be mayor yourself, one day, the way these things go."

He stood back and surveyed the youth, who was staring at him with terrified eyes, his upper lip twitching.

"It looks very odd to me, Yarwood—"

He left the sentence unfinished, leaving Yarwood a long pause in which to turn over in his mind the oddness of nothing in particular.

"Well—what do I think is odd about it, Yarwood?"

"Dunno, sir."

Kenworthy stormed at him in a voice that must have been audible in distant recesses of the police station.

"Odd, Yarwood, that you weren't with him when he did the museum. You were his ghost, his shadow, hung on his coat-tails. If we look in the records, which we will in a minute, I'll bet we shall find that you went on probation when Chick did. Got done for lifting stuff from Woolworth's when Chick did. Had Chick's girls, when he'd done with them. But suddenly you sprouted a pair of ruddy wings and a halo and left him to do the museum on his jack."

"Honest, sir, I said to him, bugger that, I said. You do that bloody lark on your tod, I said. These two will tell you—"

"All right, sit down, Yarwood. I'm glad you're not my mate. Detective superintendent will take your statement presently. If you'd told us all this three days ago, I'd have said thank you—Now—Who are these other two beauties?"

"William Burgess and Arthur Carter."

"One at a time.—William Burgess.—Up, laddie!"

Burgess was one of those who affected tight jeans, a dirty denim jacket and the hair-style of the laughing cavalier.

"Now—what's your yarn?"

"Well, sir—on the night Chick done the museum, we was walking along Wakefield Road—"

"What time of night was this?"

"Between two and three in the morning."

Kenworthy laughed like a lunatic, clasped his hands against his stomach and staggered howling about the room.

"What was that for? Taking your poodles for an airing? Or looking for dog-ends?"

He laughed again. He was red in the face. He looked as

if he were about to have a stroke. The man could act. There were genuine tears squeezing out of his eyes.

He brought out his handkerchief and wiped them.

"Well?"

"No, sir, we wasn't doing anything we shouldn't."

"It's your normal practice to go taking the air between two and three on a winter's night, is it?"

"No, sir. We was with Chick, see, and he said he was going to do the museum, and we tried to talk him out of it—"

"You'd actually teamed up with him for the job?"

"Well, sir, we had at first, I got to admit it. But that was early on, when we was talking in the *Saracen's*. It didn't seem all that clever, when it got nearer the time, not to me and Arthur, it didn't. So, I could see Arthur's thinking what I am, and, like I said, we started on Chick, working on him to turn it in."

"And then you left him to it?"

Burgess's brow lightened a little at this suggestion that at last he was possibly being believed.

"Yes, sir."

"And walked up and down in Wakefield Road until he'd done?"

"Yes, sir."

"Ready to warn him if any fuzz turned up?"

"No, sir. We'd made up our minds we wasn't going to have anything to do with it."

"You mean, if a policeman had come along that road while your friend was breaking into the museum, you'd have scarpered and left him to it? I wonder what Chick would have said about that?"

"We'd talked that over," Burgess said. "If a copper had of come, we was going to run for it, only make a bit of a row about it. It seemed only fair."

"In other words, you were accomplices. Accomplices in a burglary, and, since you knew for what purpose the weapon was wanted, accessories before the fact of murder."

"That's going a bit far," Burgess said.

"It's not going far at all. You two would be a bit young to remember the Craig and Bentley case, but it's since the war. Lord Chief Justice Goddard. They topped a laddie of your age for very little more than you've done. Topped him, Burgess."

Burgess looked as if he expected to be topped within the next few minutes.

"So I wouldn't want you to incriminate yourself, Billy. And if you've any second thoughts—"

"I can't go back now on what I've said, can I?"

"You haven't made a written statement yet, and if you do so, having been warned of the possible consequences of it, you do so of your own free will."

And then, as he saw that Burgess was about to wilt, he added, "though of course, it's bound to come out sooner or later, so it's up to you to get yourself in the clear if you can."

"I'll make a statement."

"What about you, Carter?"

The other youth agreed by momentarily closing his eyes.

"Good!—Well now, Billy—tell us what you saw."

"We saw Chick Stanway, working on the window."

"What was his technique? How did he go about it?"

"Sir, he stuck a piece of sticking plaster on the glass, then he cut out the best part of a circle with a glass-cutter, then he put a second piece of plaster on, then he lifted the circle out, then he scored the rest of the glass, then he pulled it out, then he got in through the window."

Kenworthy showed an increase of interest.

"And when he was easing the glass out, Burgess—did he pull it towards himself, or lever it inwards?"

Burgess thought for a moment.

"Pulled it towards himself," he said.

"And then what did he do with it?"

"Put it down gently on the gravel path."

"You saw a hell of a lot, didn't you, Burgess? You must have spent more time standing at the museum gates than you did walking up and down in the Wakefield Road."

"We was interested, sir. Course we was. He was our mate, wasn't he? We wanted to see how he done it, didn't we?"

"And it must have been a bloody bright night."

"There was a good moon, sir—and not much cloud about."

"Carter!"

Kenworthy wheeled on the youth who was still sitting.

"Go and stand outside the door. And you go with him, Yarwood.—Now, Billy—how big was the moon?"

"About three quarters full, sir."

"What shape was it?"

"A bit flat on the top right-hand edge."

"And where was it?"

Burgess answered as if he had not really believed his ears.

"In the bloody sky, sir."

"Sorry!" Kenworthy said. "I thought it might have been shining out of Yarwood's bum.—Where was it in the sky? High up, low down, overhead?"

"Just over the top of the trees, sir."

"All the bloody trees in Fellaby?"

"Them in the church-yard. Where the rookery is."

"Well done, Billy. A fine bit of nature-craft. Remind me to tell your scoutmaster I've passed you for your badge."

He brought Carter back, asked him the same questions and received effectively the same answers.

"Fair enough, me-laddoes. Detective superintendent Rhys will take all your statements in a few minutes. Just wait here."

Kenworthy took Rhys into the corridor.

"Congratulations!" Rhys said. "I enjoyed that. I'm glad to know that we're going to get statements in spite of your solicitude."

"Yes—and damned useful statements they're going to be.—You do see the import of these interviews, don't you?"

"I should hope so."

"It isn't what you thought when you first came to tell me that the lads were here."

"I'm not a fool," Rhys said.

"Well, you know how to go about it now, don't you, Rhys? See them separately, harry them on every sentence. Check and double-check every shade of an idea. Be nice with them one minute and bloody nasty the next, so they don't know where they stand."

"Thank you, Kenworthy. That will be a great help to me. I am for ever falling down on taking statements. In twenty-five years of experience, I have never seemed to get them right. And what about Stanway? Do you think we ought to have him in again?"

"Stanway?—Oh, yes, Stanway.—Yes, I think you might bring him in for a spot more questioning. May I leave that to you, Rhys? Wright and I are going to be busy this afternoon."

"And if it reaches a certain point, shall I charge him, Kenworthy?"

There was an optimistic timbre in Rhys's voice. It was well known in provincial forces that Kenworthy often fed in information and then stepped modestly aside to let the local officers make the final arrest and take the superficial credit. He said he did it to save himself paper work and appearances in court.

"Charge him? Oh, yes, if you're satisfied that the statements are enough to hold him on, charge him with breaking and entering. And illegal possession of a fire-arm, too, if you want to pile it on. But don't charge him with murder on the present evidence. On what you're got up to now, you can only allege intent. And superintendent—"

"Yes, superintendent?"

"Don't give him bail," Kenworthy said, and swept Wright away before Rhys could make any retort.

"Right, Shiner—quick as you can, and as unobtrusively as you can, get hold of those bits of broken window, and let's get over to the museum."

Gill was still on leave, and his senior assistant was an obliging but fussy woman who, they thought, would never leave them to get on with their work. Wright pulled away the boarding for a second time, whilst Kenworthy brought out the triangles and irregular polygons of glass and began to arrange them on a table.

"Got it all, sir?"

"About four fifths of it. Some of the splinters won't tell us much. But we've got most of the perimeter, and with that and the circle to orientate us, we shouldn't go far wrong— Damn it, I never knew jig-saws were so difficult. The trouble is, we don't know which side the picture's on."

Wright rested the sheet of plywood against the wall and came over to help.

"Shouldn't this piece be the other way up, sir?"

"Should it?—Well—You have a go."

Eventually Wright completed the composition. Kenworthy brought a tape-measure from his waistcoat pocket and began to measure the distance between the cracks, and to chart the distances on a piece of paper.

"Now, Shiner—show me where you spotted the cracks in the putty."

"They're not all very well marked, sir. And I'm afraid I spoiled a bit of it, last time I was here."

"We'll try, anyway—"

Kenworthy brought his tape and diagram to the window.

"Here's one—and here's another—"

He took measurements and applied the edge of his paper to the window-frame. Then they went back to the reconstructed pane.

"No doubt about it. Look—you can see from these little blobs of adhesive which side he worked from. I'm afraid this may be going to put Gill's laundry bill up again. You were quite right, Shiner—this was done from the inside. And those boys were lying."

Kenworthy replaced the glass in the envelope. Wright nailed back the board.

"This complicates everything, Shiner. I can't see any alternative to pulling a really dirty one on Rhys this time. I don't mind baiting him a bit—that keeps him on his mettle. But this time I'm going to have to go too far. Once he knows about this, he's going to have to release Chick. And whatever else happens, I don't want Chick released this side of midnight. On the other hand, once the lad's been charged, someone's got to eat humble pie, and that ought to be my job. Amen. So let it be. Our job is to find Barson's murderer, and if we have to rub up Rhys the wrong way into the bargain, that's just too bad. I take full responsibility for suppressing what we know about this window. And we must both keep out of everybody's sight for the rest of the day."

He looked at his watch.

"Blast! It's still only mid-afternoon. We've a hell of a lot of time to kill. Shiner—I don't want to give you an inferiority complex—but would it offend you if I say that I think I ought to handle tonight's combination of Lesueur and the Chief Constable myself?"

"Not at all, sir."

"Good! Then that will leave you free to spend the evening with Putty."

"Putty?"

"Putty. No competition tonight, see? I don't know where you'll find her. You mustn't under any circumstances go to her house. Her dad would half kill you. Make a few enquiries round the caffs, and so on. But find her you must. And I can tell you, with Chick inside, and all sorts of rumours current about the nature of the charges, she'll be beside herself. I want you to convince her of two things. Firstly, that the only way of clearing Chick is to find out the name of the real culprit. She might even manage that for us. Secondly, that it will put us on the right track if we can only find out who fed those cowboys that pack of lies. Because they didn't invent that co-ordinated stuff about the moon themselves—it was cooked up for them, and well drilled. I think it's probably even accurate—we must check up on that. Now Putty will worm that out of somebody if she has to fight for it with broken beer bottles. Get the drift, Shiner?"

"I do."

"Well—now get out of town. Get on a bus. Go and study the scenery. Only not the same bus that I shall be on. In short, Shiner—get lost!"

"On my way, sir."

· 17 ·

AFTER DREARY HOURS of buses, the streets of towns similar but inferior to Fellaby, wiping steam from the window as the dusk came down, Wright came back to the High Street ready to step into the shadows on the approach of any beat-walking policeman who might recognise him.

He knew that Kenworthy had been right to make sure that they steered clear of Rhys, Grayling and Dunne. They had no blind eyes to turn in Fellaby police-station. Once an event, a message, an arrest was logged, its timing was on permanent record for Her Majesty's Inspector of Constabulary who might descend at any moment for a routine check. They lived by the book, and the book was backed by a minute-to-minute record that could tell no lies. The moment Stanway could no longer be held, he could no longer be held. And the moment Wright or Kenworthy were confronted with their county colleagues, though there might still be subtle prevarication, there could be no lie direct. Hence there must be no confrontation.

Wright sought out Lenny, and the cripple was peering from his doorway, not more than a dozen papers left on his stand. The afternoon's history had not yet hit the headlines of a paper printed in distant Bradcaster, but there was a fudge in the Stop Press that had made an excuse for a placard.

"Things are moving," Lenny said.

"They're moving right enough in one direction."

"Lost your boss again?"

"No. I'm looking for a girl."

"Putty?"

"You know, do you?"

"It stands to sense, doesn't it? Chick's inside. Billy Burgess and Arthur Carter are inside. Larry Yarwood's been inside and has been let go again. Who'd know the truth? Putty!"

"Any idea where I might find her?"

"I don't know the number of her house, but I can tell you where it is."

"I don't think it would be a good idea to go to her house."

"I don't either. They get the wrong idea, there, when one of you blokes knocks. Usually it's to put the old man away for something or other, or because the neighbours have rung up to get a domestic row quietened down. Pots and pans flying about, on pay-night. Besides, old Pearson doesn't hold with her having men friends."

"She certainly does seem a bit young for some of the things she's mixed up in."

Lenny spat.

"Young? What's young mean? She's as old as her brain, isn't she, as old as her body? I don't what-you-might-call know her—but I've seen her often enough, and she looks to me as if she's ready for it."

"Where would you start looking for her, then, if you were me?"

Lenny considered.

"That might not be so easy, sergeant. Her friends won't be her friends any more now, will they? And none of them are using the *Saracen's Head* any more.—Course, you might go and stretch your ears in the Coconut Club. That's if you're not too particular what company you keep. I wouldn't be seen dead in there, myself."

"Thanks," Wright said. "I think I know where that is."

"Second to the left off Railway Road."

"Thanks."

Then he suddenly decided to go abundance on his confidence in Lenny.

"Know anything about Lesueur?" he asked.

Lenny put on a plum-plated pseudo-aristocratic tone. "Not the society I usually keep, sergeant."

"But you'll have heard things—"

"Bastard! Runs this town—bastard!"

"He ran Barson, too, I've heard somebody say."

"He put Barson to the top of the tree. That's common knowledge."

"And Colonel Hawley?"

"A proper gentleman. Not to be mentioned in the same breath. He got me off of doing time, Bill Hawley did."

"Oh?"

"For non-payment of fines. Collecting betting-slips, before they changed the law. I wouldn't pay up, because nothing's worse than nothing, I thought, and I thought well, I'll go and see what it's like inside. And I had them beat, by God I did. They didn't know what to do with me. Couldn't queue up for my grub. Couldn't slop out. So they put me up in the hospital. Bloody treat, it was: bars on the windows, but clean sheets and a nice little nurse, who waggled her bottom when she walked. Then Bill Hawley came back off a holiday, and found out where I was, and paid my fine, so they sent me home again, the bastards!"

"Good night, Lenny."

"Good night, sarge."

The Coconut Club was in an area basement sandwiched between a second-hand clothes shop and the local headquarters of the Transport and General Workers' Union. But Wright was saved from making an entrance by the sight of Yarwood, looking dusty and disconsolate, with one of his bottle-green epaulettes torn away, standing in the shadows outside the door. The youth started when Wright touched his shoulder.

"All right, lad, don't be scared. I don't want you this time. I want Putty."

"Putty doesn't come here any more."

"I don't blame her. Do you know where she is?"

"Dunno."

"Could she be at home, do you think?"

"Might be."

"Could you get her to come out for me, Yarwood? I want to see her. There's just a chance of getting Chick off—"

Yarwood led Wright along dismal roads parallel to the shopping streets of the town, taking short cuts through the narrow passage-ways between houses. Theme music from the evening's television programmes drifted from dimly lit

windows across cluttered back yards. Yarwood did not say
anything. He did not even speak about the direction they
were taking. Twice he turned unexpectedly to right or left,
so that Wright had to check his step suddenly and take long
strides so as not to be left behind.

Eventually Yarwood changed his gait to a long, sauntering lope, walking very close to the houses, even brushing
the window-sills of some with his elbow, and began to
whistle, loud, piercing and out of tune, a song that had
climbed the popular charts some months previously. By a
window at the end of a terrace he stood still for some
seconds, bringing his whistling up to an orgiastic climax.
Then he turned abruptly into a brick arched alley between
the houses, speaking over his shoulder to Wright for the
first time.

"Keep your feet quiet!"

They passed walled yards, down towards more houses on
their left, on their right a couple of acres of untidy allotment
gardens. At a corner of yard wall, where an unpaved lane
separated the parallel backs of houses, they came to a
standstill.

"Keep under this wall," Yarwood said, "or they'll see us
from the house."

They heard a back door open, and footsteps crossed a
yard. There was a noisy fumbling with the latch of an
outside lavatory. A few moments later, quietly and suddenly, a small figure joined them. She started back when
she saw Yarwood.

"You?—You've got a nerve! What do you want?"

Then she caught sight of Wright.

"Oh!—It's you—"

Disappointed, Wright surmised, because he was not
Kenworthy.

"If we want to help Chick," Wright said, "we've got to
work hard and fast. Can we go somewhere to talk?"

She spoke quickly to Yarwood.

"Go and get Doris to come and call for me. It's the only
way I can get out. They're watching me like hawks."

"Doris is down at the Coconut, with Stevie."

"I shall have to risk it, then. Must go and put a coat on,

though. Don't hang about here. Go right back to the Brow and wait for me on the corner."

She went into the yard, gave the noisy hinges of the lavatory door more work to do and let herself into the house. Yarwood took Wright back to the main road, within sight of Mrs. Sawyer's paper-crossed window.

"You know," Wright said, "you're going to save us an awful lot of time and trouble if you come clean."

"There's nothing to come clean about."

"You may have beaten Kenworthy and Rhys, but you'll not beat Putty."

"Putty can say what she likes. She can't alter the truth."

A courting couple passed them, on their way out of the built-up area, huddled ostentatiously together, an aggressive gesture to the world outside themselves. It seemed a very long time before Putty came—quick, brittle footsteps in the night.

"Let's go Fellaby Moor way," she said. "There won't be so many nosy parkers.—Now what's all this about? What did you want to go and put the coppers on to Chick again for? They'd finished with him, hadn't they—had him in and let him out again?"

"Putty—you've got the wrong end of the stick. We was talking, Arthur and Billy and me. And it was Billy's idea. Chick's all washed up anyway, he says. So why should we have the down on us, too?"

"Marvellous!" she said. "You were supposed to be Chick's friend."

"Yeah, but—"

"Yeah, but nothing. I reckon you're the one who thought it up, to go and grass on him. That's why they've kept Billy and Arthur and let you go."

Wright did not try to correct her false reasoning. It would be better to let her find her own devious way to a conclusion.

"Well, go on, then—what did you tell them?"

"Only what they knew already. What Chick said in Wardle's, when Barson sent his brother down."

"Well, what did you want to remind them of that for?"

"The point is," Wright interposed, "we need to know

who *told* them to spill the beans—who *fed* them the story they told."

"What story? He says he only told them what they knew already."

"Go on, Yarwood," Wright said. "Get it off your chest."

"That Chick had always said he was going to get the Luger—just as a mascot—"

Putty thought deeply. They had stopped walking, and were standing in the shadows, beyond the town's last lamp.

"Well?" she asked Wright, seeing no further line of thought.

"Yarwood will tell us the whole story, if we wait long enough. He also said that Chick had plainly said he was going to break in and get the Luger to kill Barson. That's not even true, is it?"

"Oh, yes, that's true."

She spoke with a touch of heart-felt sadness.

"It's true. Chick said it more than once, and dozens of people heard him. He was always talking big."

"In that case," Wright said, "I can only say Chick's in real trouble."

She retorted angrily.

"I know Chick's in real trouble. You haven't brought me out just to tell me that, have you?—Where's Kenworthy, anyway?"

"He's out—following up another line."

Wright was worried. Why on earth should Kenworthy think that Putty could derive any sense out of this impasse? She was only a bit of a kid. She wasn't even leaving school till Easter. And yet he had an uneasy feeling that Kenworthy would have teased a useful response from her.

"So what?" she said. "We might as well all go to bed."

"But you're not with me," Wright persevered. "Chick said he was going to get the Luger—but he didn't actually *do* the break-in, did he?"

"No. He didn't. I'm certain of that."

"How certain?"

"Dead certain. I should have known about it if he had. He couldn't have kept it to himself. And he couldn't have done it, anyway. The job was done with a glass-cutter, wasn't it?

Chick couldn't have used one of those. He's too clumsy to put an electric light bulb in without breaking it."

"But Billy and Arthur both say he did it. They say they were with him just before, tried to talk him out of it, actually stood in the Wakefield Road and saw him working on the window."

"That's just a pack of lies!"

"I know it's a pack of lies. You see, Kenworthy and I have bedrock proof that the museum wasn't broken into at all—it was broken out of, which is a totally different thing, and which Billy and Arthur weren't to know. I don't think Yarwood told more than the truth—as far as he saw it—but the other two were put up to telling a tissue of lies."

"They could have made them up for themselves," Putty said, "just to get at Chick."

"We don't think they did. It was all too carefully worked out. Details like what phase the moon was in—"

Putty stamped her foot and turned round, so that she was facing the town again.

"Billy and Arthur couldn't have thought of that," she said. "They haven't the sense. They haven't a tea-spoonful of brains between them."

"So—somebody must have drilled them in what to say."

She wheeled savagely on Yarwood.

"Who was it?"

"Honest, Putty. Billy and Arthur came to me. It was their idea from the start. I don't know anything about anyone else talking to them."

She paid no further attention to him.

"I'll soon sort this out. I'm going back to town."

And then, as the other two fell in step with her: "No. On my own. I'm going to do this my way."

"We want to get this settled tonight," Wright said. "Where shall I meet you again?"

"I'll ring you at the County Hotel. I *can* use a call-box, you know."

Wright watched her resolute figure walk with firm steps across the yellow pool of light from the first street-lamp. He looked with loathing at Yarwood, who was standing, hopeless, a couple of yards from him.

"Get out of my sight!" he said. "I've finished with you."

· 18 ·

IT WAS AFTER midnight when Kenworthy returned to the hotel. Wright was waiting up for him. Putty had still not phoned.

"I've just been over to the nick," Kenworthy said. "Rhys is still at it."

"You told him?"

"Gave him back the bits of glass."

"Did he half murder you?"

"On the contrary"—Kenworthy looked pleased with himself—"He saw the point. He had come, in a somewhat circuitous way, to some pretty clever conclusions himself. He's a steady old plodder, is Rhys, and like many another cart-horse, he can pull a bit of weight. And he's a damned good policeman. He knows I used him as a stooge to get Chick out of circulation, and he accepts that as his lot. And he took my hints about taking their statements. Burgess and Carter couldn't speak to anything outside their brief. Hence, their brief must have come from an outsider. And Yarwood wasn't in on that at all."

"But he's charged the other two with complicity in the break-in?"

"They're sweating it out in separate cells. It's a question of whose nerves will break first. And Rhys has piled the brushwood on in the usual way. He's still up, drinking station tea, waiting to see which will be the first to make a second statement."

"You know, sir, sooner or later he's going to ask us why we haven't checked the museum keys."

"We have. Before I left town this afternoon, I took that

trouble. Gill has one. The caretaker has one. They carry a spare at the town hall. It doesn't really help. Keys can be borrowed and copied. Lesueur may have kept one when he handed the premises over to the borough. Hawley may have one. We may have to do some intensive staff work on keys before we've finished. I hope not. It will be a wearisome old business. And how did you get on with Putty?"

Wright told him.

"And she's not rung yet?"

Kenworthy looked at his watch.

"I'm beginning to wish I hadn't put so much on her shoulders. She can handle the cowboys—but if she falls foul of the power behind the scenes, it will be a different matter. I'm going to phone Rhys and bring him over here."

Rhys was red in the face, as if his blood pressure was likely to be the first casualty in the battle. But he was a happy policeman; he thought he was on the verge of satisfaction.

"I don't think it will be long now. But I can't help thinking that whoever put them up to it has them on a pretty tight lead."

"Well—let them crack in their own time."

Kenworthy explained that they were waiting for Putty, and why. He also sketched in rapidly the various developments with which Rhys was unfamiliar.

"Well, if you're going to draw your bow at Lesueur," Rhys said,—"which it's pretty clear you'll have to—you don't have to apologise for keeping me in the rear rank. I'm not the one to shirk my duty, but this sort of job is best done by a Londoner."

"I've just been having dinner with Lesueur," Kenworthy said, "and the Chief Constable."

Rhys whistled.

"Incidentally, Shiner, you were very badly missed. Lady Lesueur asked most kindly after you—'that young man with the Cockney accent, who likes his food—'"

"Which reminds me, I've had damn all to eat all evening."

"Pity. We had an absolute dream of a prawn cocktail. And sliced melon, with a cherry on top. *Coquille St-*

Jacques. Aitchbone steak, two kinds of potato, including croquettes that melted in your mouth. Paw-paws and whipped cream. Stilton, really ripe, fed with port—"

"Turn it in!" Wright said.

"It was a dinner-party in a million.—I don't mean just the chuck, though that was out of this world. I mean for sheer subtlety and refinement. It was rather like a cross between tournament bridge and liar dice. Everybody knew what all the bids meant. Nobody dared call anybody else's bluff. You could pass on a pair of queens as a full house, and everybody knew what you had in your hand, but they had to accept your offer. I enjoyed myself. I let it be known, for example, that I associated Lesueur with Barson's wife. Just dropped it into the conversation that we'd called at 19 Hagley Brow. Made out I was trying to illustrate the house-pride of the poorer people here. But the reference wasn't lost on Lesueur."

"How did he take it?"

"Turned to his wife and said 'one of our long-standing tenants, dear. Quite a distinguished beauty in her youth—' almost as if he were trying to justify himself in my eyes for having seduced her."

"What did the Chief think of all this?" Rhys asked. "Did he cotton on?"

"From the very start. Quite a personality, your Chief."

"We think so. Did you get a chance to brief him in advance?"

"No. Didn't try. And didn't have to. He saw at once that I was gunning for Lesueur. And he backed me to the hilt, without once forgetting his manners as guest of honour, or dropping his guard as my superior officer. For example, Lesueur was tickled pink that you'd charged Stanway. He'd heard it on the six o'clock news. I said outright I was sure Chick hadn't done it—we were glad to give the real culprit a sense of false security and the chance to overstretch himself. The Chief met my eye across the table. Saw I was trying to get the knife well and truly in. Asked me outright if I had any evidence on which to clear Chick."

"You told him about the museum window?"

"Not on your Nelly," Kenworthy said. "Too much hangs by that. I hedged. I chose that moment to mention that

Barson had had a fancy woman in Kirby-le-Dale. Lady
Lesueur was disgusted."

"And Lesueur?"

"Knew about it already, I'll swear. Oh, he said all the
things one might have expected—scandalised surprise, and
all the right reactions. But he couldn't quite pull it off. He
was really shaken that I knew about it. There was something
just a little too suave in the way he refilled our wine-glasses.
I thought the Chief was going to wink at me.—A vintage
Moselle, too—"

He looked wickedly at Wright.

"This suggested that Lesueur had, in fact, met Warren,
whatever he may have said to Shiner on the point. I let it be
thought that I'd had it from Warren's own lips. And it went
home. It was Colonel Hawley who gave the game away—
just by an extra flicker of his eye-lids. The colonel's no
fool. He saw the way the wind was blowing, and played
into my hands in a number of little ways. Rather like
playing opposite a dummy that knows the game."

"Did Lesueur try to cover up?"

"Not really. In fact, at this point he was at his lowest ebb
of the whole evening. He didn't do himself justice at all. He
came out with a frightfully weak story. Said yes, of course,
damn it, he remembered now, ought to have known who
Shiner was talking about, but Shiner's description of him
had fallen so far short of what one might have expected
from a professional man—"

Wright screwed up a bit of paper, hurled it at a pedestal
ashtray in a corner of the room and missed.

"My next move," Kenworthy said, "was to discover
whether Warren had called on Barson, and this was rela-
tively easy. Apparently Warren and Barson had come
together to see Lesueur. That makes the blackmail angle
look even stronger."

"Don't forget, sir," Wright said, "that we were worried
about the blackmail possibility when we heard that Warren
had blown the gaff to Mrs. Sawyer. That still remains to be
explained."

"I think I know the answer to that, Shiner—but let's wait
till we see Heather's report on *Salamander Enterprises*.—
Incidentally, that might be in already—I still think there's

been blackmail about. And after I'd done with Warren, I thought I'd better go easy on Lesueur for a bit. So for the rest of the meal I stuck to general conversation. Lady K wanted my impressions of Fellaby, so I was able to turn the talk to the plans for the new High Street."

"You call that general conversation?"

"Well, it just fell out that way. Lesueur got back on form—quite an honest man, in his way. Held forth at length on the relative amenities of multiple stores and family businesses. Said quite frankly that he was afraid his own view was in open conflict with his strongest political supporters."

"Which," said Rhys, "showed the Chief the rest of the picture."

"He grasped it all right. A lesser man might have kicked me under the table."

Kenworthy looked at his watch again.

"You know, Shiner—if anything's gone wrong with your little plan, and Putty's dad decides to cut up rough, you're up the creek, my lad."

Wright looked at him in some consternation. It was often difficult to know whether Kenworthy was joking or not, but at the moment he seemed in deadly earnest.

Kenworthy turned to Rhys.

"We might have a job getting sergeant Wright off the hook."

Rhys was seldom not in earnest.

"If you ask me, both of you have been sailing pretty close to the wind, as far as this young lady is concerned—"

"What are the Moral Welfare people like in Fellaby?"

"Very co-operative."

"Get on to them in the morning. Get them to threaten a care and protection order. That'll stop the old man's mouth."

"I think it would be more to the point if we *did* ask for a care and protection order."

"Not on your life!" Kenworthy said. "Putty can look after herself.—Is the Report Centre manned all night?"

"Skeleton staff only," Rhys said. "I've taken the liberty of letting the Centre run down a bit."

"That's always a healthy sign. I'll see if Heather's managed to get that report in."

He went to the phone, and after a few seconds called for a notebook, in which he proceeded to write at great length. Rhys whispered to Wright.

"If you're really worried about something to eat, sergeant, there's all night staff in the station canteen."

"If you asked me for my second priority, I wouldn't know whether to say food or sleep. But right now my main wish is not to vacate this front seat. I don't think Kenworthy's going to lose any time over this, now Lesueur's seen his cards."

An electric bell cut across their conversation. They saw the night porter come sleepily out of his cubby-hole and cross to the street door. Wright followed a yard or two behind and saw Putty standing under the outside lamp. The porter was unsure of her. Wright leaped to let her in.

"I'm sorry—I couldn't get through by phone. All the boxes seem out of order."

Her face was tired. Her cosmetics were cheap, badly put on and stained by the sweat and stresses of the evening. She was an odd mixture of callow adolescence and weary maturity.

"Did you get what you went for?"

Wright took her up to the mezzanine lounge, where the others were sitting.

"I got something," she said. "Not much, though. I only hope it means more to you than it does to me."

"Tell us about it, Putty."

Kenworthy spoke to her in fatherly tones. It was easy to see why she had become so attached to him.

"That lot!" she said, making a gesture which seemed to take in the whole of Fellaby. "That lot!—They want their heads tested. It's taken me till now to get a ha'porth of sense out of them."

She wiped her forehead with the back of her hand, a small hand, with coarse skin and an unsightly wart.

"It goes back to the night Chick left the gang and Riley took over. Some of them wanted to go over to Sal's caff, where Webbe and his crowd hang out, and teach them a lesson. Riley said no. He said the cops had played pretty square with them for once, and he wasn't pushing his luck. But some of them had already set out—Billy and Arthur amongst them, of course. Riley sent a couple after them, and these two saw Billy and Arthur taken in tow by a man in a car. He came up behind them, got out and talked to them, then drove them off somewhere."

She reached for her cheap little handbag.

"Nobody know who he was, of course?"

"That lot! They don't know anything. And when it comes to a description, they must be half blind, too."

She brought out a tiny little notebook, decorated with a picture of a Siamese cat on the front cover. Wright was interested to see her handwriting: small round letters, sloping backwards, immature and laborious.

"Not a big man. Not a little man. Thickset. Car coat, with a fur collar, expensive—not less than thirty pounds. No hat. Black hair, parted nearly in the middle, but not quite, and plastered down flat on either side."

"Warren!" Kenworthy said. "Putty—you couldn't have done better."

He turned to the others.

"The cheek of it—the very day I'd talked to him in his office.—Now, Putty—we've got to think of getting you home."

"I can't. I daren't. I'm dead scared."

"We can look after you. I'll send a policewoman to have a word with your mother. You slipped out to give us some information that you knew was vital—"

"That wouldn't help. They wouldn't want to be on your side, even in a thing like this."

"They might, Putty. This isn't chicken-feed."

"No!"

"I'll see if the porter can fix you up with a room for the night. Then in the morning we can get one of the welfare officers to go into things for you.—They're sensible types, Putty—not do-gooders, or anything like that."

She subsided. She was too tired to argue. And tomorrow was tomorrow.

Kenworthy fetched the porter.

"You're lucky, miss. No. 17 didn't turn up. These commercials!"

Putty turned on the stairs.

"What about Chick?"

"We'll let him out in the morning—after he's had some breakfast. Not much point in turning him out in the middle of the night, is there?"

"When can I see him?"

"Come round to the station and have breakfast with him. Would you like that?—Good night, Putty. You've saved the day for us—and for Chick."

He picked up his notebook.

"Heather's produced another of his semi-miracles. And I'm not surprised to learn that Lesueur has no connection at all with *Salamander Enterprises*. One can never be sure of tracing all the share-holders—there's always a floating population, as it were. But Heather knows where most of the money is, and Lesueur couldn't have had more than a five or six per cent holding—which wouldn't have interested him."

He brought out his pipe. They were in for another long session.

"This is no more than we had expected. But what might surprise you is that *Salamander* is very small fry indeed, minimal capital, almost on the rocks, and a reputation so bad that they wouldn't have got a look-in on the Fellaby redevelopment. Even Lesueur couldn't had resuscitated them without rousing suspicion.—And so, Shiner, I come back to something that's been in my mind ever since you gave me your support on what you learned from inspector Cook—about Barson in Germany. There was something characteristically Barson in all that. It nearly led to his own undoing, and the undoing of those about him. It's this: Barson couldn't be content with someone else's racket, even if it were a going concern. He was both big-headed and tightly blinkered enough to think he could out-Lesueur Lesueur. And my reading of events is this: when he contacted Sturgess in Kirby-le-Dale, it was to try to make his own settlement for Fellaby High Street—to sell out Lesueur and cash in himself."

Kenworthy blew his nose.

"Now we can understand why Mrs. Sturgess said they were afraid of Colonel Hawley. Of course they were.

Hawley represented the establishment—and they were agin the government.—Does all this make sense?"

"Possibly," Rhys said, "but there's a heavy element of speculation in it.".

"True. But let's see where it may lead us.—When Gill put Barson into Warren's hands, he gave him a good deal more than Barson's garden-path. I'm quite sure that Warren quickly saw that there wasn't much to be made out of Barson. Barson's never been a thrifty man. What money's come his way, he's spent on his idea of good living: his wife can't even afford to pay the grocer's bill. So Warren concentrates on Lesueur."

"If that is so, why should he take Barson with him when he called on Lesueur?"

"It may have been because Lesueur was not easy of access, and Barson had the open sesame. I think it's more likely that he used a confrontation—as you or I would—to get an admission out of Lesueur."

"But surely he was damaging his whole prospects by putting the garden-path at Gill's disposal?"

"Not at all. By bringing Barson into disrepute—or, rather, by letting someone else bring Barson into disrepute—he automatically gave credence to the big stuff that would follow."

"It's a wonder Warren wasn't the one who was killed."

"Perhaps he would have been, before long. Perhaps it nearly came to that, and he got Barson first."

"I'm sorry to keep reminding you of this," Wright said, "but we still don't know why Warren blurted out what he did to Mrs. Sawyer."

"No. But we can make an intelligent guess. Warren saw Barson to tell him the chips were down. Barson blustered. He would. Not reasonable—but Barson wasn't a reasonable man. So Warren has to show him—and Lesueur—that he really means business. He blows the Barson-Sturgess liaison into the open. Then he takes Barson to see Lesueur."

"So you think," Rhys said, "that Warren ultimately killed Barson in self-defence? How, then, did he get hold of the Luger? Might not Lesueur be the murderer? To destroy Barson as Warren's evidence? Or Hawley, acting as always as Lesueur's trouble-shooter?"

"Hawley's shot plenty of trouble for Lesueur in his time. And we also know, from the slum-clearance appeal, that there were times when he jibbed at shooting trouble. He'd jib at shooting a man on Lesueur's behalf.—At the moment, I wouldn't like to choose between Warren and Lesueur. If I have a strong preference for settling on Warren, that's all the more reason why I propose to leave that gentleman to you."

"We're a long way from knowing the truth," Rhys said.

"We must get that in the morning. For one thing, we've now pushed our suspects as far as they can go. If we don't settle with them immediately, this case will go on for months. What's more important, I've been away from my home comforts too long already. I shall, if you'll pardon the intrusion, make myself responsible for Lesueur tomorrow morning—"

"You're very welcome," Rhys said.

"If there's a charge against him, I'll try to keep him on ice till you're round.—Because I propose to give you this case. I'm heartily sick of it. It leaves a very nasty taste in my mouth."

"Thank you very much."

"In exchange for a promise. You'll be handling Warren in Bradcaster while I'm at Fellaby Moor. If you can charge him with murder, do so without waiting for me. But if you can't do him for murder, do him for something else. I want you to promise you'll break him. Warren's been going on too long."

"I'll do my best."

"If you can pull it off, they might even make you Chief Constable of Bradcaster."

"And what about me?" Wright asked. "Fellaby Moor Hall with you?"

"No. I want you to stay behind here. To mop up. Anything that needs mopping up. Including settling our hotel bills and having our cases at the station in time for the 3:47. Because the 3:47 is our last chance of a connection that will put us in our own beds tomorrow night. And I've had more than enough of Fellaby."

· 19 ·

AFTER KENWORTHY AND Rhys had departed on their missions, Wright found something sad and nostalgic about the streets of Fellaby. He had come to know the place extraordinarily well. He felt as familiar with the tradesmen in the principal shops of the High Street as he was with those of his own suburban Broadway.

And today they were leaving. He ought to have learned enough by now of Kenworthy's eccentricities not to doubt the point. If Kenworthy said they were catching the 3:47 train, they were catching the 3:47 train. Wright had been foolhardy enough to bring up the subject at breakfast, and Kenworthy had fixed him with a savage glare.

"Fallen in love with this place, have you?"

"No, sir, but—"

"Whatever else we may or may not have achieved, we must have succeeded in putting our man on the *qui vive*. If we don't strike today, we lose the initiative."

Without counting them he gave Wright a handful of pound notes with which to pay his share of the bill. The girl at the reception desk showed no surprise that they were leaving. She assumed, as did the rest of Fellaby at this moment, that the arrest of Stanway closed the file.

But Chick had already gone, when Wright reached the police station. Putty had left with him, and no one knew for certain where they had gone. And Kenworthy, who had preceded his sergeant by some twenty minutes, was just coming out of Grayling's office, finishing a conversation in the open doorway.

A constable's head bobbed round an office door.

"Sergeant—there's a couple asking to see someone about the Barson case. A Mr. and Mrs. Sturgess—"

"I'd like to sit in on this for a few minutes," Kenworthy said.

But he made it obvious that he did not propose to conduct the interview. He did not even sit down, but stood near the door, with his hand on the knob.

Mrs. Sturgess still had her hair over one shoulder, but she had dressed soberly, and looked as if she had had a sleepless night. Brian Sturgess looked washed out, too: a tall man, with curly oiled hair, who was passing into fleshiness from what might have been a handsome, lady-killing youth.

He began with a forced laugh.

"Thought I'd better come and get things sorted out, before the local bobby claps his hand on my shoulder. That would be bad for business."

"Half the story—or all of it?" Wright asked Mrs. Sturgess.

"I've told Brian everything," she said in an affectedly faint voice.

Her husband put his hand hammishly on her shoulder.

"I've told her: I couldn't really expect to keep this kind of goings-on in half the family. This has done us a lot of good, sergeant—brought us together, you might say."

"How often did you meet Barson?" Wright asked him.

"Twice."

"Both times at your home?"

"Yes. He wouldn't come to the office, or meet me in public, for fear of compromising his plans."

"Which were?"

"The first time, he was throwing the name of Sir Howard Lesueur about. I think you already have a rough idea of the proposition."

"And the second time?"

"He dropped Sir Howard. Lesueur was just a blind to get me interested. He was quite open about it. He wanted to branch out on his own."

"Is it the sort of business you'd have been glad to handle?"

"On Lesueur's money, yes. On our own capital, and on

what little Barson could have put into it, it would have been out of the question."

"You told him so?"

"No. I played him along for a bit. There were other little ventures I thought he might back."

"Just a quickie," Kenworthy interrupted. "Did you tell this to Warren, Mrs. Sturgess?"

"More or less. He seemed to know already that Barson was trying to double-cross Lesueur. I can see now that it was a shot in the dark to get more out of me."

"Thank you," Kenworthy said, letting himself out of the door. "—See you, sergeant—"

Wright persevered with the interview, but it was more for the sake of form than in the hope of discovering anything new. There was nothing to be added to the picture of Warren, and Lesueur was a somewhat legendary figure, frankly beyond Sturgess's horizon. And nothing fresh emerged about Barson, except a caricature of commercial ineptitude, which Sturgess drew with scornful relish.

Wright asked again if either of the Sturgesses had visited Fellaby before. Sturgess's denial was as vehement as his wife's had been.

"You didn't just nip over here to cast your own eye over the development site?"

"I've already told you, I didn't give this a second thought, as far as *Salamander* was concerned. Look here, sergeant—I thought you had a youngster under lock and key?"

"He's already been released. The case is still wide open, Mr. Sturgess."

Sturgess looked bewildered.

"We know where to find you, if we want you, Mr. Sturgess. If you think of anything else you think we ought to know, you know how to contact us."

The Sturgesses crept out like souls in limbo. Wright closed his notebook. There was hardly any point in recording the interview. Kenworthy had already seized the only relevant point, and that merely confirmed his own hypothesis.

"Sarge!"

The constable's head appeared again.

"Yes?"

"Someone else to see you. I suggested he should wait for superintendent Kenworthy, but he seemed to want to get on with it. Says it's urgent. He refuses to talk to any of our own officers."

Wright looked at the portly, elderly man who stood hesitant in the doorway, wrapped in a thick grey overcoat, with a home-knitted woollen scarf visible under its collar. He was hatless, his iron grey hair was cut short all over his large head, and he was wearing round, tortoiseshell-rimmed spectacles of pre-war pattern.

"Do come in," Wright said.

The newcomer held out his hand.

"You're one of the officers from Scotland Yard? Working on this terrible business of alderman Barson? I always like to know who it is I'm dealing with."

He spoke with deliberation, in full, north country vowels.

"I'm sergeant Wright. Superintendent Kenworthy is out at the moment. He's not likely to be back before lunch, perhaps not even then. I know he's heavily committed all day."

"Aye, well, I expect you've all got plenty to do, and I'll not keep you long. Only I haven't been able to sleep for nights. I had to come and see someone about it. My name's Durkin—Albert Durkin—Councillor Albert Durkin. You'll have heard of me. People will have talked."

Wright indicated facially that he had heard of the man.

"Aye, well, it'll depend on who you've talked to, what you'll have heard. I'm a self-educated man, sergeant. I've served the welfare of this borough to the best of my ability, almost since I was a boy. And a few of them may have laughed at me, because I've never had the taste or the training for wrapping things up in fine-sounding phrases. But I was always taught to be honest."

He put his hand inside his coat and brought out two foolscap envelopes, stamped and addressed in the meticulous copper-plate of the Edwardian copy-books.

"I'm a ruined man, sergeant Wright. This one's to the town clerk, resigning from the Council. This one's to my own party secretary, apologising for the harm I'll have done them—and likewise resigning—after more than forty years, thirty-eight of them in one unpaid office or another."

He left the letters lying on the table.

"I'd half a mind to ask you to post them for me. But that's something I must do for myself."

Durkin picked up the letters and tapped a nervous tattoo with their edges.

"It's useless dithering like this," he said. "One minute you're one of the town's leading citizens—they were just talking of making me an alderman, you know. The next moment, you find you've cut all the ground from under your own feet. I'll come to the point, sergeant.—It's those paving-slabs, from the Highway Department—I had a dozen of them for my own garden-path."

"At the same time as alderman Barson?"

"Aye."

Wright felt obliged to give him a formal verbal caution.

"Though actually, this will have to go to inspector Malpas. He's handling this particular case."

"Aye—Malpas."

Durkin stared in front of him.

"Well—Malpas and I know each other well enough. Known each other for years.—I'll ask you to do one thing for me, if you wouldn't mind.—Have a word with Malpas first, will you—just so I don't have to start from the beginning with him?"

"I'll do that, certainly."

Wright wondered whether this were an instance where Kenworthy might have operated the Nelson touch. Malpas had discovered no ramifications. The men on the corporation lorry had said nothing about Durkin. The quantity surveyor had asked for no additional cases to be taken into consideration. Durkin's confession was the only thing that could lead to his undoing. But the peccadillo was too near to the heart of the main case to be canalised into oblivion. Once it arrived in Malpas's hands, there could only be one outcome. And, in any case, there was no telling what the town clerk's internal researches might reveal.

"You'll be thinking it's funny," Durkin said, "me working hand in glove with Barson. I expect you'll know that we two were always going hammer and tongs at each other. But we weren't fools enough not to be on speaking terms, when there was no political issue between us—which was rare enough. Barson was always friendly with the yard foreman. He offered me those slabs—oh, don't think I'm trying to shelter behind him—I'm telling you this, just so you'll be able to carry away a fair angle on my character—for what that's worth. Barson said they were faulty material— couldn't be used. Couldn't be returned to the manufacturers, either. And no charge to the rate-payers. I let myself believe it, as a sop to my conscience—but I knew, in my heart of hearts, of course, it wasn't true. And it's clear to me now, why Barson cut me in on it—though may the good Lord forgive me for suggesting such a thing. If the deal had gone wrong, he'd either stopped the mouths of the political opposition—or he'd have brought my side down with him."

"We've been left with no illusions about Barson," Wright said.

"No, perhaps not. But I was his critic, not his judge. I knew Barson and his background long before he came into politics, even before he went into the army. It was rough, sergeant Wright. It was the sort of thing, thank God, that we're coming near to extirpating from English society. It was the sort of thing that would have made most men join my party. I used to tell Barson he belonged to us. He didn't see it that way. I'm sure he was wrong, but he had to be where he thought he could be most active. He had to hit out—hit out hard and all the time. Often he wasn't too particular who got hurt in the process. Neither was I, in my early days. It's a strange thing, sergeant Wright, what a similarity you might find between Barson and this lad who killed him. I've known Chick Stanway since he played in the gutter—Barson's gutter."

"The news hasn't travelled round, yet, then," Wright said. "We're no longer holding Stanway."

"Oh?—Does that mean you've got someone else? Or are you as far from it as ever?"

"We have some ideas."

Durkin looked into space. Wright could see that his mind was running over the possibilities. A man like Durkin knew Fellaby probably better than the town clerk—better than

Grayling, Dunne, Putty, Lenny, or the rest of them put together.

"It's no use," he said suddenly. "I don't belong here any more."

"Nevertheless, there are one or two highways and by-ways on which I'd value your opinion."

"You can have it—for what it's worth."

"Did this man Warren—the famous character in the green hat—call on you?"

"No. I'd have told him where to go. It's fairly obvious what he was up to."

"Oh?"

"Collecting gossip."

"On whose behalf?"

"His own, like as not."

"You know him, do you?"

"I know of him. We're near enough to Bradcaster."

"Blackmail, do you think?"

"What else?"

Suddenly, Wright knew that he was a man he could trust.

"Do you think he might have been blackmailing Lesueur?" he asked.

"Now, young man, you know that asking a question like that can only bring out the worst in me."

"All the same—"

"He might."

"About what?"

"I'm not guessing."

"About Lesueur and Barson and the redevelopment plan for the High Street? Would that surprise you?"

Durkin cleared his throat contemptuously.

"We knew all about that, on our side. We'd have been ready for them, sergeant."

"Would you say Colonel Hawley was tarred with the same brush as Lesueur?"

Durkin gave a little chuckle.

"My bitterest enemy, in theory. I've said Bill Hawley is the best socialist the Tories have got. He's saved many a man from the worst Lesueur might have done for him."

"Did you know that Barson's affairs at home were not all they might have been?"

"I don't listen to gossip."

"That he was keeping a woman at Kirby-le-Dale?"

"It wouldn't surprise me. But I'd regard it as Barson's business, not mine."

"Warren made it his business, too. So he did the fact that Barson was married to Lesueur's illegitimate daughter."

"She wasn't," Durkin said, looking enigmatic.

"Who wasn't?"

"Enid Sawyer wasn't Lesueur's illegitimate daughter. A lot of people thought that. I know different."

"And what do you know?"

"I've already told you, sergeant—I don't gossip."

"But this is the one link in the chain that we lack."

"The last knot you want for the rope, you mean.— Besides, it doesn't follow, sergeant."

"What doesn't follow?"

"That Enid's father killed Barson."

"No. But it's an interesting thought."

"That's why I'm saying nowt."

Durkin brought out the north country negative with an impact of decisive finality. And Wright knew that it was final.

"Because too much trouble in this world is caused, sergeant, by people having interesting thoughts. Can we go and see Dick Malpas now?"

The old man rose, simple-minded and obstinate, as determined to keep his piece of vital information to himself as he was to rule *Finis* at the end of his political career.

"You wait here," Wright said. "I'll go and see the inspector."

Kenworthy would know for a certainty whether to put the pressure on Durkin. And if the pressure had to be put on, Kenworthy was the one to do it. Wright went to see Malpas, and the inspector was irritated at this unexpected postscript to what he had considered a tidy little case.

"Oh, gawd!" he said, with abortive comicality. "Does the town clerk know?"

"Not yet."

"This will break his heart. All right, sergeant. Thank you. I'll go up and see Albert."

There was nothing more for Wright to do in the police

station. He went over to the Report Centre and found the skeleton staff idle almost to the point of immobility. It was time the Report Centre was wound up; but such decisions were not for Wright even to consider.

He wondered whether Durkin himself might be the girl's father. But even allowing for the oddest quirks in the old man's character, that would make it difficult to account for Barson's meteoric rise on the wrong side of the political fence.

The town clerk, even? Sphinx-like and detached, yet shaping the outcome of every real decision made in Fellaby, he was the confidant and constitutional adviser of both sides. Servant of right and left equally, he owed nothing to either of them. Even Barson had had the sense never to attack Belfield.—Barson had never attacked Belfield.—And Belfield had been enigmatic about Enid Barson's parentage.—He was a man whom even Barson respected—even Durkin—

Wright was cut short in his speculation by a telephone call from Kenworthy. Speaking from Fellaby Moor Hall on a bad line, the superintendent seemed remote and unusually officious.

"Sergeant—go and check that Sir Howard was drinking after hours in the *Griffin* on the night of the murder."

So Lesueur was claiming an alibi. And it did not seem a very promising assignment. No publican was going to stick his neck out. And it was unlikely that his memory would be any too precise about his own law-breaking.

The *Griffin* was a pretentious, artificial pub with contemporary decorations on the corner of a council estate that Wright had not visited before. The landlord looked in his engagement book.—Yes, there had been a ward party political meeting that evening, in the private bar. And Lesueur had certainly been there. It was most unusual that he should come out to one of the estates like this. But it was not unheard-of, especially when there was a bit of bother on. And there were warring factions out here, that were splitting the party down the middle. Some of the women— Oh, the meeting had broken up at about a quarter to ten, but some of the men had stayed on to drink a jar or two. After hours? Well, of course, no drinks were served after, but some of the men wanted to stay on and talk. Well, it went on till just after midnight. They'd probably have been there half the night, if Bill Hawley hadn't caught the landlord's eye and broken the party up. A bloody nuisance, if you'd pardon the term, because the landlord and his wife needed their bed as much as anyone else. But you had to keep an eye on the future, when you were dealing with men like Lesueur.

Wright returned to the town. Lesueur was in the clear. So was Colonel Hawley. Perhaps Rhys was making better progress with Warren.

There was nothing else to do, either at the Report Centre or the police station. The morning came lamely to its end. Wright thought it as good a time as any to carry their bags from the hotel to the station. But as he handed them in at the drowsy left-luggage office, he reflected that he more than half expected to be trudging back to the hotel with them in the early evening.

· 20 ·

KENWORTHY RETURNED WHILST Wright was queueing for liver and bacon at the police cafeteria counter.

"You checked at the *Griffin*?"

"Yes. Lesueur was there throughout the operative period."

"Not that he needed that to clear him," Kenworthy said.

Wright told him what he had learned from Durkin.

"It makes you think, doesn't it, Shiner?"

"It certainly does, sir."

"I wonder if it makes you think what it makes me think?"

"That depends on what you think, sir."

Wright did not want to be cornered into voicing a suspicion that probably Kenworthy would laugh to scorn. But Kenworthy was unwilling to make the first move, either.

"There must be hundreds of decent folk in Fellaby, Shiner. Not, of course, that it's often our lot to move about amongst decent people. I'm hoping that Rhys will have been able to pin it on to Warren. Otherwise, I'm afraid we're going to have to pin it on one of the few men in Fellaby decent enough to have murdered Barson."

"That's what I'm afraid of, too, sir."

"Well, come along, Shiner—who are you thinking of? As the one who will shortly be reporting to your superiors on the way you're making out, I have the right to insist on an answer."

Wright moistened his lips.

"I was thinking of the town clerk, sir."

"You were, were you? Well, I hope you're wrong."

"He's been in Fellaby long enough to have fathered the child, sir. He has enough influence behind the scenes, I think, to have helped Barson on his way. He could easily have kept Mrs. Sawyer in her creature comforts. He'd have had no difficulty at all in putting his hands on a key to the museum. And twice he has retreated when the Lesueur-Sawyer relationship cropped up in conversation."

"Possible," Kenworthy said. "One thing—it was obvious from the moment that I started this morning that Lesueur didn't do it. I checked his alibi, because he insisted that I should. But by that time he almost had me apologising for having suspected him. I certainly wouldn't enjoy questioning him if he were the guilty party. The man's a mind-reader. He made no bones about it, Shiner. He knew what I'd come for. Of course, the talk at his dinner-party can have left him in little doubt. But I had to admire the way he squared up to me."

Kenworthy speared peas with his fork.

"He said at the outset, without any enquiry, that he wasn't the father of Enid Barson but that he could hardly expect me to believe that; Fellaby had an *idée fixe* about it. And he volunteered that Warren asked him for a cool two thousand to hush up the redevelopment plot. As if, Lesueur said, the same thing wasn't going on in dozens of councils throughout the country, whatever the colour of the majority party. And no law was being broken, as long as Barson himself had no undeclared financial interest in any transaction that was pending. Naturally, Lesueur hoped that his friends on the council would put business into his hands, when they legitimately could. He firmly believes it is to the benefit of the community at large whenever they do so. But to allege corruption—to *prove* corruption—is a very different thing from launching an attack on political grounds. He practically challenged me to prove anything—which, of course, I can't. Lesueur is safe, and he knows it. Moreover, he has already given up hope of gaining anything from the development scheme. It would be incompatible with the private interests of his supporters. He admits he's disappointed. He openly says he could have made fifty thousand clear—but Fellaby will get its shopping precinct, under the arcade of the civic centre, and the little man will be protected.—What animal surrendered this liver, do you think—a rhino?"

"Did he know that Barson was trying to go it alone in the High Street?"

"He knew that before Warren did. A man like Lesueur has to know everything. He laughed himself silly at the thought. It would have done him more good than harm, he said, if Barson had gone ahead and broken himself. Barson's big mistake was Mrs. Sturgess. One shouldn't mix pleasure and business, Lesueur said—and he ought to know."

"Did he tell you why Warren and Barson called on him together?"

"For the reasons I advanced last night: access and confrontation—with the accent on confrontation."

"Did he give you any reason for fixing Barson's preferment all along the line?"

"The same argument that he produced to you, when you asked him the same question—only watered down and wrapped up a bit for my superior intelligence.—Barson had his uses—until he forgot who was feeding him."

"Can I get you a sweet, sir?"

"I hope you see one important thing," Kenworthy said, when Wright had disposed of the tray. "Warren's blackmail bid failed. He was left with his earnings from Gill, and has been sailing close to some bitter winds. Barson was of no further use to him. But I doubt whether Barson had finished with Warren. Warren brought out all the juggernaut in Barson, and I think Barson was determined to break him. So there's always hope, Shiner."

A second shift of policemen came in for their midday meal. Kenworthy finished a plate of trifle, ate cheese and biscuits, then smoked and lapsed into long periods of silence. The canteen began to clear. Kenworthy showed no sign of wanting to move.

"Do you think," Wright asked him, "I ought to have put the pressure on Durkin?"

Kenworthy blinked lazily.

"Sheer waste of time," he said.

"You wouldn't think of having a go at him yourself, if the thing goes on for another day or two?"

"Won't be necessary," Kenworthy said.

The hands of the clock went on inexorably from two to a quarter past, then half past the hour.

"Where the hell has Rhys got to?"

"I expect Warren will demand a fair amount of time, sir."

"Nonsense. Either Rhys will have got him in the first five minutes, or it will be a war of attrition for days—with Warren winning—"

"Rhys will know that, surely."

Kenworthy made no reply at all. At twenty minutes to three, Rhys came down the stairs.

"Well?" Kenworthy asked.

"He's inside. Locked in the cells in Bradcaster main police station, much to the joy of several senior officers there. But not on a murder ticket."

"What, then?"

"Conspiracy to pervert the course of justice—"

Kenworthy frowned.

"You begged me to break him. I don't know what other charge I could have preferred. Warren has a cast-iron alibi for the vital night. He was at a charity ball in Bradcaster, together with at least half a dozen of the Bradcaster inspectors, who can vouch for him as no one else could.— And we do know that he talked to those lads."

"We know he talked to them—that's all we do know. What did he have to say about it?"

"Collecting evidence. Making a bid to solve the Barson case as a free-lance."

"Very probably true," Kenworthy said. "And Burgess and Carter haven't cracked yet, have they? Couldn't some-one else, as well as Warren, have talked to them? Someone with a stronger influence on them than Warren?"

"So I've got a beauty on my plate—with Warren already closeted with his solicitor—"

"It isn't that that's worrying me," Kenworthy said. "It's where we go from here. You must have picked up quite a few other odds and ends from Warren. It wouldn't surprise me if he knows who the murderer is."

"He *does* know who the murderer is. He offered to sell me the information, in exchange for dropping my charges, the cheeky sod."

"Well, he's an accessory, then. He can't hold on to that piece of information for ever."

"He can deny that he ever mentioned it. Warren's confident that he'll shake off this charge. So am I, now you've changed your mind about him—"

"I haven't. Now listen—he offered to sell you the murderer's name—"

"At his own price. We can't possibly—"

"I know we can't possibly!—But if he made you an offer like that, he must have offered you some token of confidence."

"He did. He says he has the museum key—in a safe deposit in Bradcaster. He says he picked it up from a bed of reeds, on the edge of the canal, and that it bears irrefutable identity marks."

"Well, that's it, then!"

Kenworthy sprang to life.

"You hold on there while I do some phoning."

"What's he on about now?" Rhys asked Wright. "Doesn't tell a man much, does he?"

"He tells me next to nothing."

"I didn't believe Warren about this damned key."

"Evidently Kenworthy does."

"I only hope he knows what he's doing."

To alleviate the Welshman's misery, Wright told him about Durkin.

"Poor bloody Malpas!" Rhys said.

When Kenworthy came back to their table, he said nothing at all to them about the nature of his errand. Instead, he returned to Warren and the perversion of justice charge.

"I shouldn't worry too much about that," he said. "You'll have to drop it, of course—but you'll have a better one, because Lesueur is prepared to go the whole hog with a blackmail rap. I don't care for the likes of Lesueur, but he has guts, and he doesn't like Warren. And with all the talk there's been about this case, he'll welcome a chance to clear his name."

"Well—that's a relief.—But it doesn't help us to get the murderer."

"The key does."

"I don't see that the key's any use, until we have the murderer in the dock."

"He will be."

"I wish you wouldn't talk in bloody riddles, man."

Kenworthy patted him paternally on the arm.

"I promised you, didn't I, that I'd leave you to gather up the crumbs?"

"I see no crumbs."

"Well—we can talk on the way to the station. And if I haven't finished by the time we get there, you can get a ticket to the first stop and come with us. That's Arnotfield. It takes just six minutes. If I couldn't solve a case like this in six minutes, I'd consider myself nothing but a burden on the tax-payer."

All of which, Wright thought, was just so much bull on the part of Kenworthy, for the superintendent did not so much as open his mouth on the way to the station, with Rhys tramping at his side, panting like an exasperated cart-horse. And there was not the suspicion of a smile on Kenworthy's face, not a twinkle in his eye, not even a surreptitious wink for Shiner. And even when they arrived at the station, and Wright had collected their bags, and they were standing on the platform, waiting for the train, all Kenworthy could do was prattle aimlessly about the tourist posters, pointing to towns of which his wife had received picture postcards, and recommending hotels in which Rhys had no interest.

The 3:47 drew in, late and grubby, and they found a first-class compartment to themselves. A whistle blew, and they were sucked into the station tunnel, with its smoke-caked brick-work. Then they were accelerating alongside the canal, the hulk of Wardle's ruin falling back beside a grey stone bridge, and they saw the roofs and chimneys of the Carlton estate. Soon, they were crossing a brook spanned by a wooden foot-bridge.

"Before the industrial revolution, Shiner, this must have been rather a lovely county."

"Superintendent Kenworthy," Rhys pleaded, "we have three and three quarter minutes left. And my ticket is only as far as Arnotfield."

"Oh, yes—Well, I rang the murderer up and asked him to meet you in the forecourt of Arnotfield station. So it would have been a waste of the tax-payer's money if you'd booked any further."

"And you assume that he's going to keep this extraordinary appointment?"

"He said he would. Very eagerly, I am told. For I did not actually speak to him myself. That would have given the game away. I got a friend of mine in Bradcaster to make the call—and to say that he was speaking from Warren's office. To say that Warren himself would be at Arnotfield—to hand over a key—at a price.—Oh, and I've arranged for a couple of quite strong young plain-clothes men to be inconspicuous but handy—just in case."

"You've left me a modicum of filling in to do myself, haven't you?"

"Not a lot. I made sure the telephone call was monitored and recorded. The very fact that our man is there at all gives you your lever. Plus the other odd little pieces that will drop into place when you see who it is."

The coarse grass of the hills bulged away in overlapping folds to the moors of the horizon. The driver began to brake for Arnotfield.

"Well, you'll see in a minute," Kenworthy said. "The only man in Fellaby decent enough to murder the man who double-crossed his daughter. No—sit still—keep your head back. We don't want him to see us too soon."

Wright was sitting in the worst position of the three to get a reasonable view of the station. But he caught sight of the mud-spattered paint-work of a red shooting-brake, and standing by its bonnet the unmistakable figure of Colonel Hawley.

"You see," Kenworthy said, "like the rest of Fellaby, we made the mistake of assuming that when Bill Hawley delivered the Christmas goodies at number 19, he was doing it on Lesueur's account. It might help you to know that he drove Lesueur to the *Griffin* on the night in question—and called to pick him up afterwards. If you want any further—"

But Rhys had bounded out of the train before it stopped. Two young men in mufti were sauntering inconsequentially up the station drive.

For the next few miles there was scarcely a break between the conurbations. A faint orange ball of sun hung in the industrial murk over the rows of terrace houses.

"For God's sake let's get back to the bloody Smoke," Kenworthy said.